BEYOND EVIDENCE

Emma L Clapperton

Dedication

Dedicated to and in memory of

Elaine Clapperton
17th January 1968 - 31st August 2012
Wherever you are, I hope that you can read this.

Copyright

Createspace
7290 Investment Drive Suite B
North Charleston SC 29418
Unites States
Contact the author for permissions.
Second Edition

ISBN 9781484017463
Cover design by Allen Theobold
Image supplied by Susan K Dailey

Acknowledgments

I would like to thank everyone who supported me in the writing process of this book, it did not go unnoticed.

I would especially like to thank Maxine for coming up with a title – one of your many crazy dreams has certainly left a mark.

Louise, for doing the edits – your advice really helped me in the final process.

Donna, for doing the original cover and even though it didn't end up as the final piece it still means so much – my best friend in the whole world who I don't know where I would be without.

All of the fabulous writers out there who have offered continual support and advice through the world of social networking – you are all amazing.

Margaret Sarah Bechtel for your continued patience and hard work, even when it drove us both crazy you were still willing to push on.

J. B. Sullivan for writing the blurb, it has been a real attraction to the story. Thank you.

Joseph Eastwood for my first edition cover- it served the book well.

Allen Theobold for designing the cover for the second edition. It is very fitting to the story.

Casey Kelleher for all of her wonderful online advice on publishing, I know I drove you crazy but I am thankful for your time and patience.

Thanks to David Leese for your contacts.

Thanks to Mark Richards for your contacts and author advice.

Thanks to Lee Brook for your patience and hard work.

My Mum and Dad for making me believe from a young age that I could be anything that I wanted to be – thank you.

My wonderful Gran – just for being Gran.

And last but certainly not least, my partner Chris. I don't know how he has managed to put up with the constant sound of the laptop keyboard and my obsessive need to write. You have been so supportive and full of encouragement when I thought I couldn't do it. Lovington X

One

Wrong Place, Wrong time

She remembered the race that she had taken part in at her primary seven sports day back in 1997 and remembered thinking, *You can do this Rebecca, you can win this and show them all that you're not the fat slob that they say you are. Keep going you can do it.*

She had put on a little more weight than she should have and wasn't the fittest in her class. The other kids knew this too and they weren't quiet about it either.

"Fatty!" they would call her as she passed them in the corridor at school. She was sick of the taunting and name calling that she decided to prove them all wrong and try her hardest to win the two hundred meter race in the primary seven sports day. It was just before school broke for the summer holiday and the sun was splitting the sky. Not even a hint of breath was in the air. The whistle sounded at the start of the race and Rebecca took off like a bullet from a gun. She could see from the corner of her eye that she was slightly ahead of the rest of the participants. All she kept thinking was that her legs were going to buckle under the feeling of jelly inside them. But she was so god damned determined to prove that she could beat them and their evil taunting. She was determined that they couldn't hurt her anymore.

That was the exact thought that was going on in her head this night, the night of July 31st 2010. It was a typical summer night in Glasgow city centre, perfect for a night out after a hard days work with the girl's. Life was going great at the moment for Rebecca. Working in Tesco's wasn't the best job in the world but it paid for her nights out, her rented flat which she shared with her best friend Caroline and her beloved Ford Fiesta.

That night in the pub was like any other normal night. She had decided to get all dressed up and make herself feel good about her appearance. She hadn't felt good about herself in a long time. She had finally slimmed down to a size ten and had been working herself ragged in the gym every moment she could.

"Are you absolutely sure it's not too short?" she asked her friend Caroline whilst gazing into the stand alone mirror.

"Oh my god would you stop? I've told you a thousand times you look great. And anyway you shouldn't care about what other people think of you Rebecca, it's your body and as long as you're happy then that's all that matters," Caroline said with sincere honesty in her tone. Rebecca gave a sigh and glanced at herself in the mirror once more. She was a very pretty twenty- four year old woman. Her long loose brunette curls hung perfectly around her heart shaped face and down her back. Her skin was sun kissed and hazel eyes glimmered under the light. She gazed in the mirror and for the first time in a long time she actually agreed with Caroline.

She wore a long black dress with one shoulder sleeve and a slit up each side of the leg. Long gold costume necklaces hung from her neck and she pulled her hair around one side of her face to let it hang over her left shoulder.

The girls left their flat on Great Western Road and made their way to the pub in the city centre. It was a hot night and the girls were excited to be having some work free time together.

On arrival to the bar named 'My House' Caroline immediately noticed a man standing alone at the bar and he was staring at Rebecca as if he knew her. He smiled at Rebecca as she entered the door but she hadn't noticed him. Caroline began motioning a glance over to the bar at Rebecca and when she looked over she noticed the man who was around her age, watching her intently.

7

He was tall, about 6ft 1" and he had dark, scruffy looking hair, a bit like Liam Gallagher's from Oasis, but shorter and glasses. He had one day old stubble and dark clothing on with a black leather jacket.

Strange fashion for the middle of July, Rebecca thought.

He looked at Rebecca with a mysterious stranger manner. Rebecca did think he was good looking but she also felt very reserved about him. Something just didn't feel right. She took her eyes off him as Caroline took her aside. "He is so into you," Caroline almost shouted over the music with excitement in her voice.

"Nah, I'm not sure. He seems a bit strange," Rebecca said with a little uncertainty in her voice.

"Ok well there are plenty of guys out tonight, we'll find you one honey," Caroline giggled.

"I'm not looking for one!" Rebecca gave a slight smile to lighten it but still remained deadly serious. "Men complicate things."

"Yes, yes ok. Well do you want to go somewhere else?" said Caroline, but toward the end of the sentence she was looking beyond Rebecca and when she turned to see what Caroline was looking at she immediately found herself standing face to face with the man from the bar!

"Hi I'm Ross," he said in a very deep nervous sounding voice, "Any chance I could buy you a drink?"

Oh shit, what do I do now? Thanks Caroline! she thought to herself, "Erm, thanks but I'm just having a drink with my friend tonight, maybe another time?" Rebecca trailed off when she noticed Caroline walking away.

"Oh, excuse me please," she said to Ross before chasing after Caroline in a panic to be left alone with a stranger that she wasn't interested in. "Caroline what the hell are you doing?"

Rebecca could clearly see that Caroline had spotted her on-off boyfriend standing outside the pub casually chatting to another girl. She knew immediately that she probably wouldn't see Caroline again until the next morning. She laughed then remembered the man she had abruptly left standing, rejected at the other end of the bar. Even though she knew instantly that she was not interested in him (or any other man for that matter) she felt bad, so decided to go over and apologise. But when she got there he was waiting for her with a drink in hand.

"I hope you don't mind but I saw you drinking this earlier and I decided to get another for you. The bar guy said it's a Cosmopolitan, I hope it's the right one," he said a little softer this time, "I realise you declined my offer at first but I noticed that your friend has other pressing matters to attend to." He made an inverted comas sign with his fingers and smiled a bright white smile.

Rebecca didn't know what to do or think. If she accepted the drink then that may be seen as saying that she is attracted to him and then he may get the wrong impression. Or if she refused it he may get offended or hurt and she would have nobody there to back her up or give her an excuse to leave. *I over think things too much*, she thought to herself.

"Well...?" said Ross offering the glass of red liquid to her.

She looked at the glass and then at him, "Ok then, just one. Thank you."

He handed her the glass and she took a sip. She watched him as she drank the red liquid and wondered if she had been too quick to judge him. After all she didn't know anything about him. Was that a good thing or a bad thing? She finished the cocktail and excused herself to go to the bathroom.

"I'll be right back" she said, thinking about just picking up her coat and calling it a night.

"I'll get another one for you if you like?" said Ross.

He said it in a way that was more like a statement rather than a question. Rebecca just smiled and made her way to the bathroom.

The butterflies in her stomach were going crazy and she didn't know if it was excitement or something else. The night went on and Rebecca found herself relaxing a little more. Ross was actually quite pleasant, he asked lots of questions, and to Rebecca it seemed like he was interested to know all about her. His skin was pale, but he had dark eyes, which seemed unusual to her. To her they should've been blue. He seemed a nice enough guy. Why not give him a chance? When all said and done she wasn't the biggest risk taker in the world. What's the worst that could happen?

It was midnight and Rebecca was sitting on a bar stool next to Ross at the end of the bar talking about work, friends, family, holidays and other "date" type conversation. She wondered if that's what it had turned into...a date?

Rebecca suddenly felt very tired and her head was beginning to ache.

"Ross it was lovely talking to you but I'm going to call it a night, I'm tired and I'm working a shift tomorrow," she smiled.

"Ok, well let me at least walk you home?" he said sounding a little disappointed.

Already he was off the stool and helping her on with her coat. Rebecca smiled again and staggered slightly.

"Are you ok?" Ross asked sounding concerned.

"Erm yeah I think so. I think the best thing for me is my bed," she gave a quiet laugh.

They were on the street outside the pub and Rebecca began feeling woozy. They began walking down the not so busy street in the city centre. Rebecca thought the reason for this was probably because there were still two weeks left before pay day. That would be to do with the current financial climate and everything that goes with it.

Rebecca suddenly realised that she didn't recognise the streets that she was walking along with the friendly stranger she had met in the pub. She also thought to herself that they had both been very quiet and been walking for about ten minutes or so longer than it took to get to her flat from the pub where she had been drinking the cocktails. She began to think about how tired she had suddenly become and the now eye watering headache that seemed to be travelling down the back of her head into her neck. Ross was walking unusually fast for walking someone home and when she thought about it, he was more so pulling Rebecca by the wrist than just kindly seeing her home. It wasn't long before she realised that she was in danger of being attacked by the 'friendly' stranger that she had said from the beginning she wasn't interested in. Had he put something in the drink? Come to think of it, he had bought the drink for her without her witnessing it. Rebecca's thoughts began to panic her.

He must have put something in my drink, she thought to herself. She remained as calm as she could and tried to clear her mind so she could concentrate on getting away from him.

"I think I'll be fine from here thanks," she said as normally as possible.

Ross said absolutely nothing, he just continued dragging her along the road, which was absolutely deserted.

How the hell do I get myself out of this? she thought to herself as she tried to keep up with his speed. They were walking so fast that she could hear his breath coming in quick rasps. His touch made her feel sick to her stomach and her whole body was pulsing. She didn't know if that were to do with any sort of drug he may have put in that cocktail or if it was adrenaline rushing through her veins, it was probably both.

The next thing Rebecca knew she was being dragged down an alleyway and she began screaming. Not word's, or at least she didn't think she was trying to form any sentences, she just wanted to make some hellish noise in the hope that someone would hear her and come to her aid. Every time she attempted to scream a pain surged from the back of her head to the bottom of her spine but she tried to ignore it. What was to come would be worse, she guessed. She pulled and punched with all her might and he resisted her physical pleas. Rebecca didn't know how she managed it with all the fatigue that she was feeling but she managed to loosen his grip and make a run for it. She had no idea where she was and the heels on her shoes snapped with the thud of each step but she didn't care, she just kept running. Everything around her seemed blurred but the adrenaline kept her going. He wasn't far behind her. She could hear the heaviness of his breath, which made her shiver knowing what he had been thinking as he dragged her down that dark, rat infested alley.

He was calling after her in a creepy, playful voice. "Rebecca, come on now, you know that the headache will stop you dead in you tracks eventually. Why not save yourself the energy and just give up?"

That's when Rebecca began thinking about the primary seven sports day back in 1997. There was no way that she would let the bullies think that she would give up that race because she was overweight, or fat as they called her. Although to be fair, kids are just kids.

They probably didn't realise the hurt and damage that they were causing at the time. But this monster did. He knew exactly what he was doing the minute that he had tampered with her drink. It's what he had had planned the minute he set his eyes on her in the pub. She began to think that she should have followed her initial instinct. She didn't like the look of him, but Caroline put it in her head that he was attracted to her. And a girl can't help feeling flattered. She pushed the thoughts out of her head and concentrated on running as fast as she could. She could feel a slight breeze on her face as she ran through the dark streets of now what seemed like the outskirts of town, which she did not recognise at all.

Her head thumped like it was being battered with a brick and then wondered if that may be one of things that would happen to her if he caught her. She could hear the distant sound of traffic and a little hint of relief ran through her. If only she could make it closer to the motorway ahead then she may have a glimmer of hope that someone would see her and scare off the psycho behind her. She could hear him, closer now, could almost feel his breath on the back of her neck. This sent shivers of fear right through her whole body. She could feel the fear in her veins, it made her blood run cold. She could see the traffic on the motorway now, but still had no idea which part of town she was in, but she didn't care. If she could just flag down a taxi at least, Caroline could pay at the other end, that's if she had even made her way home. Would a taxi even stop on a motorway? It might if there were a hard shoulder.

Then she knew it was all over. The monster that had been pursuing her for what seemed like hours was now on top of her, but she had fallen face down when he had leaped on her from behind. She was pretty sure that she had created quite a distance between them whilst running. Maybe she was right, because it felt like he had taken a jump to reach her as he had almost landed directly on top of her head.

The scream didn't want to leave her throat. She tried and tried, but then realised it couldn't because he was squeezing her throat so hard that she couldn't get a breath. His hands were cold and she could smell cigarette smoke from them. She knew she was going to die and she wasn't ready for that. But at least she couldn't see the crazed eyes of the beast that literally was squeezing the life out of her. She still fought though. But he had the advantage of being in control in how restricted her movements were.

She closed her eyes and thought of who would find her. Hopefully it wouldn't take too long. She didn't want her parents to have to identify a body that had been left to decompose so badly that it was unidentifiable.

In fact, maybe that would be the better option. If she was unidentifiable then maybe the police wouldn't let them see her. She preferred that thought. Her parents were the last faces she saw in her mind before everything went black...

Two

Soul Mates

Patrick McLaughlin knew that he was different from all the other kids his age, or anyone else for that matter. He could see things others couldn't and hear strange voices over the echoes of the football match going on a break times or in the school cafeteria. Those voices and the visions always seemed louder and more vivid in busy places, as if they knew that it was harder to get through. Sometimes Patrick recognised a face in the rush hour in his head, or felt comfort in the particular voices that rang in his ears. As he got older and the years went on he seemed to understand the purpose of the voices and the faces. Although it took a long time to find the off switch.

In the beginning, Patrick was just a normal five year old boy who played football, army games and all the other things little boys did with their friends. But he always had that extra something that nobody else did. He didn't particularly think it had a name at that age, he just assumed everyone else could do what he could, until he started school. When the other kids realised that he would talk to people that weren't visually there some of the kids would avoid him or make fun of him.

That's when he realised that he was different. He often wondered if he was the same as his biological parents and maybe they had the same abilities as he did. Patrick had been adopted as a newborn baby so he knew nothing about his birth parents. He would make up scenarios in his head sometimes, where he and his birth parents would sit around a table talking to spirits that had passed and wanted to give a message to a loved one. Patrick did not have the desire to meet them but his scenarios gave meaning to his ability to speak to the dead.

Any spirit could visit Patrick at any time and sometimes he found it good company. If the spirit was not good company however, they could sometimes get angry if they hadn't had a good soul whilst they were on earth, he would try to block it from his mind. He particularly liked it when his Grandpa came to visit him, which was his father's father.

He would say things like, "Patrick, you'll understand that one day, all this has happened for a reason." Patrick didn't understand at the time but he would later in life.

One cold February morning of 1984, Patrick was sitting at the desk by his primary three classroom door. His teacher, Miss Donald was giving a maths lesson. The class was freezing cold and it had been snowing non stop for a whole week. Patrick wasn't paying the slightest bit of attention as he didn't have a big interest in maths. That wasn't the only reason why, though. He could sense something, he had a feeling in the pit of his stomach that a big change was coming. That sensation of butterflies in his stomach just got stronger the more the clock ticked by.

As he gazed out of the window where his desk was situated at the back of the class he saw the large flakes of snow flutter down on to the grass where later in the spring, the daffodils would begin to sprout. The sky was completely white and even though he could hear the murmur of Miss Donald's voice at the front of the class, he could feel the silence outdoors. As he fell deeper in to his daydream, he continued to watch the snow fall with some snowflakes bigger than others. Some flew directly towards the window from where he gazed and others swirled around the sky before settling on a spot to land. He looked out to as far as his sight would allow him and he could pick out the silhouette of a man. He knew instantly that it was his Grandpa, which made him smile. Patrick watched as he made his way over to the window, like any normal human would he walked through the snow but behind him there were no footprints. Even though his movement imitated walking, his Grandpa's form seemed to float gently, as if his own spirit carried him through the cold wintery air.

Grandpa? Patrick spoke in his mind, never daring to allow the class to hear him.

Hello Patrick, his Grandpa smiled gently as he finally reached the window.

Patrick blinked and in that split second, he felt his Grandpa's presence on the other side of his body, sitting next to him on the empty chair.

I like when you visit, it makes me happy.

Me too, his Grandpa replied. *You feel it, don't you?*

Yes but I don't know what it is. Do you know?

Patrick knew that his Grandpa was referring to the change in the atmosphere, the feeling that something big was going to happen but not knowing what that change was.

Yes, I do know. But you must experience it on your own. If I tell you what it is, then you may not be able to fulfil your purpose.

Patrick felt confused but he decided that his Grandpa always knew best and that he would never keep anything from him that could harm him.

Ok. Can you at least tell me when? He tried to make his young voice sound brave at the unknown but there was still a quiver of fear hidden under the front.

Yes, it is going to happen today and very soon.

As he looked at Patrick with a gentle glowing smile, his appearance began to fade. Patrick did not like this part of his Grandpa's visits but he knew that he could not stay. As Patrick returned his gaze to the window, he saw his Grandpa walking back in the direction which he had come from, again imitating the action of walking but somehow appearing to float. Patricks heart ached each time his Grandpa left, it felt like he had died all over again. But as time passed and his grief slowly lessened he had learned how to deal with it. He knew it was easier for him to cope with the loss as he was still able to talk to his Grandpa and feel the comfort of his presence every now and again. Patrick understood that his Dad and his Gran were still incredibly sad about their loss and the reason for this was the knowing that they would never talk to him again, touch him or hear him. But Patrick could and for a long time, would hear him and see him. The comfort of this was soothing since his family were still very much in the grieving process. For Patrick it could become quite overwhelming at times, especially since he was still a child. In Patricks head, he felt older and more knowledgeable but on the outside he was merely a child who had lost a grandparent, one who he was very close with and who knew his secret.

He did not know how to behave when it came to his Grandpa's death. He did not think that it would be good for his own dad to see him upset as it may set off his own emotions however, he did not want it to seem as though he was unaffected by the situation. Thinking in these ways made Patrick grow up quicker than he should have, allowing his ability to develop alongside his early maturity.

Patricks attention clicked back into reality when the head teacher, Mr Parkinson came into the class. The feeling in his stomach abruptly stopped. Behind Mr Parkinson was a girl, the same age as him, or roughly there about.

"Miss Donald, this is Jodie Jenkins." Mr Parkinson led Jodie over to Miss Donalds desk and began to write something on a piece of paper.

Whilst Mr Parkinson was writing, Patrick couldn't help but look at Jodie in absolute knowing that the feeling he had been having and what his Grandpa had talked about was to do with her. The big change that was running through his head as the clock ticked by each second seemed to make the sound of a click just as soon as Jodie had stepped into the room. The strange thing was that Jodie was looking at Patrick with the exact same expression on her face as he had. To him she glowed.

"Class, this is Jodie Jenkins, she is our newest pupil to the class so make her feel as welcome as she should be please." Miss Donald smiled at Jodie and ushered her over to the seat that every child in the class had avoided.

Words were not exchanged during the rest of the lesson, it was only during lunch time that Patrick spoke to Jodie for the first time.

"My name is Patrick," he said as they gathered their belonging to head to the cafeteria.

Jodie glanced at him and said, "I know."

Patrick paused for a moment and immediately understood what the click in his head had meant when he first set eyes on her. *She can do what I can do!*

Jodie glanced at him and as she did she raised the side of her mouth, releasing a very small smile. *I sure can.*

The school cafeteria was buzzing with children every which way you turned. The noise was loud and echoed words bounced off the walls. Unless anyone focused on two particular children having a conversation, no one would be able to define the nature of the hundreds of conversations that were taking part around Patrick and Jodie.

"So, why did you move school?" Patrick asked.

"I was bullied in my last school because people didn't understand why I was different. They all thought I was weird and picked on me for talking to myself. It got so bad that I didn't want to go to school."

Jodie stared out at the other children in the large hall while she spoke. "That's when I realised that I should use my brain to talk to them rather than actually talk out loud," she said as she nibbled on a sandwich that she had taken out of her lunch box.

Patrick could see that Jodie felt sad about what had happened to her but he could hear her thoughts telling him that she was glad that she had met someone else who was exactly like her.

Days passed and Jodie and Patrick spent a lot of time together, at school, after school and any other time in between. Not a lot of conversation took place, or so it would seem to those around them. Their conversations were kept private between their senses and their own minds.

Patrick had learned that Jodie's senses weren't as similar as his in the way of vision. Jodie was also more able to switch off, but mostly she would keep her senses open. She felt that she was given this sense purposefully and that she would be able to use it to someone else's advantage at some point in her life.

Patrick talked to her about his Grandpa and all the things that he said about Patrick having a purpose too. Jodie felt comfortable around Patrick and she understood him like she understood herself.

"I think that we were meant to meet Patrick," Jodie said as they played on the swings next to Patricks house.

"I think so too," he replied as he manoeuvred his legs to reach the highest height he could. The air swooshed passed his ears as he gained height and fell back down again. He could see his Grandpa sitting on the roundabout opposite him and he was smiling.

"My Grandpa is over there," Patrick said.

"He is?" Jodie couldn't see him.

"Yep, he is smiling. He told me about you."

"He told you about *me*?" she sounded surprised.

Patrick stopped the swing and sat still next to Jodie. "Well, not *about* you but he said that he knew that a big change was coming. I could feel it that day, in class just before you came in. My Grandpa came to see me and he said that he could feel that something was going to happen and he knew what it was but I had to figure it out for myself."

His Grandpa was gone again.

"Well I am glad that it was me. Although I don't think that I have been much of a change, do you?" Jodie asked curiously.

"You will be, but I don't think that whatever it is will happen for a while. I think that we were supposed to meet for a reason and we will find out why in the future."

He is right you know. In the future you will know exactly why you were supposed to be together, Patricks Grandpa spoke to Jodie. Patrick heard it too and they both smiled.

Jodie only ever heard voices, she never saw the spirits themselves. She liked to listen to the voices. Mostly they described how they missed their human life and that they would love to come back to do all of the things they hadn't done that they regretted. The voices varied in age from children as young as seven to the elderly. There were voices of health, disease and illness but all of the voices that Jodie sensed were those that led happy lives.

She had never experienced any unpleasant spirits.

Jodie discovered however that Patricks senses were not always as pleasant the way her own were.

Three

Twenty six years later

Patrick lay in bed. He tossed and turned, threw the covers off and pulled them on, opened the window, then closed the window. He repeated this several times before he decided to give up trying to sleep. He got out of bed and turned to look at his sleeping fiancée.

Jodie hadn't moved an inch during all of Patrick's sleepless commotion. He bent down and kissed her slightly on the forehead and then crept quietly from their bedroom, down the hall into the living room. He decided to keep the lights off, he figured that it might help him relax and hopefully he would fall asleep on the couch. He opened the sliding glass door and went out onto the balcony. He took a deep breath and looked out at the express way that his building faced onto. The road was deserted, well it *was* four o'clock in the morning. There was a slight breeze in the early morning air. Patrick took the cigarette pack off of the table and slid one out. He studied the lone cigarette for a moment, wondering if lack of sleep was worth a smoke. He had been on and off smoking for a couple of months now, but the last few weeks were like hell without them. He kept a pack in his apartment at all times. He thought that it be better to have them there in his opinion. It would be better to have one cigarette than be seriously stressed about trying not to smoke at all. Jodie always found this amusing.

"It's just your way of not giving it up completely!" she would laugh.

He decided his lack of sleep over the last few weeks definitely was worth it and lit the cigarette. He drew deep on the tip and savoured the nicotine that would sail through his body within moments and held it for a few seconds.

This will calm my nerves surely, he thought to himself. He exhaled slowly. Patrick's sleepless mind began to wander now that he felt more relaxed. He thought about the dreams he had been having and about the random women in them. They were women he had never met before, women he did not recognise.

He thought about them, all three of them. Their distressed mannerisms, tattered appearance and obvious fear in their eyes were what made him question the dreams. Of course, everybody dreams at night, but not everybody's dreams kept them awake for most of the night. He felt almost sure that it had to be something to do with his ability to communicate with the dead but he had never experienced it this way and in mass volume like this before. One of the women was around his age. She was small, about 5ft 1" and well dressed and she would just appear to him. She wouldn't say anything but just look at him, however as the nights went on her appearance and manner changed. Her clothing became tattered, her hair was hanging all around her face and she had bruising all around her neck and shoulders. She reached out to him and tried to speak, but all that came out was a croaking, gasping sound. The weeks drew on and as the dreams continued a second woman had appeared. At first she was just like the first woman, very well dressed and pretty. She looked in her late twenties or early thirties at a push. Again no words were spoken, just looks exchanged and as the nights went on, her appearance and manner also changed with her hair hanging around her face and her clothing soiled with what seemed like grit and oil, as if she had fallen on the pavement on a rainy day.

Her injuries seemed similar, but she also had scrapes and grazes on her face. She reached out for Patrick too, as if asking for some kind of help. Her voice was almost non existent. She clawed at her throat as if she were suffocating and gasping for air. The dreams didn't frighten him as such, they just woke him at all times of the night and got his mind ticking about who they were and why, night after night they continued to contaminate his sleep.

He drew deep on the cigarette again and turned to face the sliding glass door, pushing the faces from his thoughts. Patrick put the cigarette out in the ashtray and went back inside. He lay down on the sofa and closed his eyes. Having a smoke had worked, he felt very relaxed and sleepy. As he was drifting off to that place between awake and sleep, he heard an unfamiliar voice draw out his name. It was a raspy voice, almost like someone with a bad throat infection or laryngitis.

Patrick.

He opened his eyes and sat up straight on the couch. Everything looked the same. The room was of medium size for a city apartment. The sofa was positioned in the corner of the sitting room and there was a large rectangular mirror on the wall above it. The television was on the opposite wall and a glass coffee table sat in the middle of the room.

Something felt different. He was cold due to leaving the sliding door open by a quarter of the way. It was July but it was also Scotland, the seasons don't play by the rules here. He stood up and took the blanket off the back of the sofa and wrapped it around himself as he sat back down. He felt a slight breeze on the back of his neck and the hairs stood on end so suddenly that he stood back up immediately. Patrick told himself it was because he had left the door open. He was facing the television and when he looked at it there was a face looking back at him, it was the face of the first woman who had been in his dreams. He couldn't decide whether he had actually fallen asleep on the couch and this was another dream or if this were his reality in all its fine form.

Her face was partly covered by her hair which seemed wet and straggly. As he looked on, his stomach was beginning to do somersaults and he felt slight nausea setting in. He spun around quickly to see if the woman was behind him, where she should be in the reflection. Before he could do anything the face reappeared in the mirror which he now faced, with the most expressionless look on her face. Patrick had never felt so frozen with fright but unusually he didn't feel any different. It wasn't like in the films where the character see's a ghost and the temperature drops and you can see your breath in front of you. The room was of normal temperature and he definitely couldn't see his breath in front of him. He tried to stay as calm as possible but he couldn't move. He was routed to the spot with fear. He had encountered spirits appearing to him many times before, but never something so graphic and sudden like this. He took the deepest breath he could so he could shout out for Jodie, whilst keeping his eyes on the woman in the mirror. She seemed to be getting closer, as if walking out of the mirror toward him. Patrick was absolutely helpless with fear of not knowing what was going on, his body began to shake and he was breaking out in a cold sweat. The woman was no longer in the mirror. She was standing by the edge of the couch, her head was slumped forward but her eyes were on Patrick. She took slow, eerie steps, closer and closer. A hand was placed upon Patrick's shoulder and he leaped two feet in the air.

"Wow Patrick it's me," Jodie spoke with a startle in her voice at his response.

"Wh, wh, where is she?" he stammered.

"Who baby? Where is who?"

"The woman," Patrick was now walking around the room putting on all of the small lamps.

"Patrick it's just us here. Are you ok? You must have had a nightmare," Jodie spoke with calm a manner.

Patrick thought to himself at that moment. He shouldn't be getting so jumpy at this sort of thing, he'd dealt with it since he was a child. But he had never in his life felt so on edge about spirits before. He couldn't get her face out of his mind. She was making him shiver at the thought of it. Those dead eyes looking up at him, her pale and beaten face made him feel nauseous again.

Patrick realised he was walking around in circles in the sitting room and Jodie was looking at him with concern more than fear. He stopped his panicked walk and sat down on the edge of the couch where the women had stood before Jodie had disturbed her.

"Can't you feel her? You have a spiritual sense too Jodie, can't you feel a presence? She...they have been here for weeks."

Jodie sat down slowly on the cushion next to the arm of the couch and took his hand.

"No babe, strange as it seems for me not to sense this sort of stuff, I really don't see or hear anything."

Patrick stood up and walked back out to the balcony to catch his breath. It was now approaching five a.m and he was wide awake with the entire goings on in his head. Daylight was setting in and he looked out on to the expressway again. There were only a handful of cars and a few delivery trucks, quietly whizzing past the apartments where Patrick stood. The sun was rising slowly to the right as he looked out and there was a haze of cloud all around the buildings that stood beyond the road. The clouds seemed to burn out the higher up he looked and the sky was a whitish blue colour. He thought how peaceful it would be up there. If only he could get some peace for a few hours so he could sleep and get his head together.

He turned so his back was to the road and called into Jodie who was still sitting on the cushion next to the arm of the couch, "I'm going to head out for a bit, just a walk to clear my head, I have something to post anyway and I'll pick up a newspaper and some rolls on the way in."

Jodie looked up and just smiled. She wanted to take him in her arms and comfort him. She had never seen him react this way about his ability to see and hear things before. It scared her deeply.

"Ok, I'm going back to bed for a bit. Take your keys in case I'm asleep when you get back." He walked past Jodie and stopped to kiss her on the forehead before leaving the sitting room. Patrick picked up his cigarettes from the table and went to the bedroom to change into jeans and a t-shirt. As he left the apartment he quietly closed the front door behind him.

Four
The Turner's

The kettle began to whistle on the hob. It was an ear piercing sound that he was sure no one else enjoyed. It reminded him of the way his mother would make tea in the mornings before he had to leave to go to school. He knew most people had electrical kettles nowadays but he was happy enough to use the boil on the hob type. He poured the boiling water into his coffee mug and stirred. His mind went back about twelve hours and he was positive someone would have found her by now. He looked at the photograph of his mother in the frame on the small kitchen wall and said aloud, "See mum, I'm making it better."

Ross Turner thought about the clothing he had gotten rid of in the last eight weeks. Three black shirts and three pairs of trouser which he had put into black bin liners and discarded at the local tip, where most people got rid of the rubbish they no longer needed in their lives. His bet was that the Police would never think to look there if they ever got a lead on their suspect.

Hundreds of people probably dumped their rubbish in that tip every day. Even if they did get a lead, they would never find any traces of those dirty whores on him if he had discarded of the evidence. He picked up the newspaper he had bought earlier that morning and saw the headline, 'Third female found dead in city.'

He sipped at the coffee he had poured for himself.

Well isn't that sad. What's the world coming to with one less whore? he thought with a sadistic smirk as he read the rest of the article.

The girls face was on the front page, just a small one taken from her facebook profile. She was pretty, with brunette hair which curled around her face. She had hazel brown eyes, sun shimmered skin and a pretty smile stretched across her small face.

"Hmm, no name yet I see. Well I'm sure we will have something for you soon mum!" Ross said aloud as he flicked the page and began reading something on the other side about house prices falling by a further 0.5% due to the economic climate.

He flicked again, reading the rest of the newspaper, as if the news on the front page were just news. To everyone else in Scotland that morning it would be, but to Ross it was yesterday's news. Or last nights anyway! Ross Turner was a thirty year old single man who lived on his own in a flat in the Partick area of Glasgow. It was a sandstone building which had stood for years. It had two bedrooms however he only used one for himself, he wasn't one for flat sharing. He much preferred his own company. Life had dealt him a bad hand over the years and he had learned to be his own best friend and to trust no one. He was fast becoming a man who was hell bent on revenge for his mother, Maria Turner.

Ross Turner had grown up in and around the North of Glasgow all his life. He lived with both his parents, until he was old enough to choose to get away from his abusive father.

As a child Ross' father subjected him to the sight of young, undignified women rolling through the door with him at all hours of the morning. Ross knew exactly why they were there and so did his mother. These women disgusted Ross. They would come into his home with his drunken father stinking of booze and cigarettes and disappear upstairs for an hour or so. When they left his father would beat Maria black and blue until he got tired and went to bed. His name was Billy Turner. Ross absolutely despised his father in the end. He would never forget the screams and pleas from his mother as Billy Turner vented his drunken state on Maria.

As a child, Ross would stick his fingers in his ears once those dirty women left his home because he knew what was coming next. The beatings became few and far between as Ross reached his middle teens. Ross threatened his father with the Police if he beat his mother and for the majority of the time it worked, but there would be the occasional night where Billy Turner had had one too many and Ross wasn't there to help Maria. Ross left school and went to university for a three year course to undertake a degree in photography and make up artistry and whilst he was away Billy Turner wreaked havoc on poor Maria Turner.

This time he was in such a drunken rage that he raped her and broke her collar bone and as Maria tried to get away from Billy, she ran from the bedroom to the top of the stairs and as she descended Billy pushed her and she tumbled to the bottom causing her to break her ankle. He kept her cooped up in the bedroom like an animal for weeks on end, giving her paracetamol for the pain in her ankle and collar bone. He didn't dare call an ambulance. That would have gotten him into trouble and he wasn't prepared to go to jail. The women still came and went most days. Maria had no idea who they were. Not prostitutes surely, he didn't have that much money. But he did have a charm that only Maria could see through. Maybe these women just fell at his feet the minute he opened his mouth. In all fairness that's how she ended up marrying him.

Maria didn't have anyway of contacting anyone, Billy had blacked out the windows and cut off the telephone in the bedroom. All she had was painkillers on a four hourly basis, water and food three times per day. Maria felt like she was in prison at that time. But she knew that Ross was due home within the following two weeks after his first year of university and once he saw what had been happening he would deal with it, he wasn't a little boy anymore.

Those next two weeks were like hell. Her broken ankle was not healing and her neck was causing her unbelievable pain. Billy was drinking in the excess of one and a half bottles of vodka everyday and he tortured Maria, everyday until a few days before Ross returned.

Maria was raped, sometimes twice per day and was force fed the food he was giving her to keep her alive. She felt like an injured animal that the vets were refusing to put out of its misery!

On the evening of May 3rd 2007, Billy had fallen into a drunken state and had left a full packet of painkillers by the side of the bed. Maria stared at them for what seemed like an eternity. She thought about all of the wasted years she had spent with the monster who was Billy Turner. Supposed to be her loving husband, in sickness and in health, for better or for worse!

Billy Turner was without doubt sick in the head and Maria was one hundred percent certain that things couldn't get any worse. Maria struggled to reach over and opened the drawer in her bedside table. She took out a small pad of paper and a pen and began to write;

Ross, I am so sorry that it has come to this. I lie here and I think about everything I could have done in my life to make yours better as you were growing up. I should have left your father years ago, but it was easier to stay. I want you to get away from your father, as far away as you can before he hurts you the way he has hurt me for the past twenty odd years. I don't blame the alcohol, I blame the hidden personality that the alcohol brought out of him. I cannot go on Ross, if I did leave, I would always be looking over my shoulder and I do not want you living your life trying to protect me! I love you very much Ross and don't you ever ever forget that. I will always be with you. Mum x

Maria folded up the short note and put it on the bedside table. She opened the pack of painkillers and with shaking hands she emptied them onto the bedding. She took the glass of water in her hand that Billy had "so kindly" left for her and she took as many pills as she could swallow in one go.

Meanwhile, Billy Turner slept drunkenly in the room beneath her. Ross returned home the next day to find Billy sat on the single recliner chair in the living room of the house. He was sat forward with his elbows resting on his knees and his head hung down facing the floor.

"Dad, it stinks in here," Ross said as he opened the curtains of the big bay windows. He turned to face Billy who was now standing. He was grey in colour and swayed from side to side.

"Hung over are we?" Ross asked, knowing the answer already. Billy said nothing as Ross waited for a reply. His eyes were bloodshot due to consumption of alcohol and crying. Ross felt his stomach lurch, like a thousand butterflies were whizzing around his intestines.

"What is it?" Ross didn't take his eyes off Billy.

"I'm sorry son." Billy picked up a bottle of vodka from the nest of tables next to the single recliner but it was empty.

He looked at the bottle then threw it down onto the carpet. Ross dropped his backpack, which made a loud thud and thundered upstairs to the bedroom. He threw Maria and Billy's bedroom door open to find Maria tucked up in bed as though she were sleeping which gave the butterflies in his stomach instant relief, but as he walked around to her side of the bed he felt utter devastation when he realised she was dead. She lay there completely lifeless and she had no colour in her face. Her eyes were closed.

Ross sobbed as he lifted the duvet to cover her face when he saw severe bruising to her neck and shoulder. He immediately realised that she had a broken collar bone. His devastation turned to sheer rage and he raced downstairs taking two at a time and burst into the living room where Billy was sat back on the single recliner swigging at another bottle of vodka.

"You evil, disgusting bastard!" Ross screamed and flew across the room. He began punching the living day lights out of Billy as he sat there like a lump of lard taking his beating. Ross stopped and pulled the vodka out of Billy's hands, "This make it acceptable does it?" He waved the bottle in Billy's face. "Does this precious bottle of vodka make the last twenty years ok to you?" Ross threw the bottle of vodka at the marble fire place and it shattered into a million pieces, spraying vodka everywhere.

Billy could see the rage in Ross' eyes.

"I didn't kill her Ross, she did that herself!" Billy slurred. He had tears rolling down his face. Not tears of a grieving husband but tears of a man who had worry tearing through him. He knew there was no way out of this.

"Don't you dare cry! You didn't give two shits about her or me for that matter. Why did you marry her if you didn't love her? Why did you make her life so fucking miserable, bringing back all those dirty disgusting excuses for women for all those years? Why didn't you just love the family you had?" Ross took a breath in between the sobs of anger and frustration.

"I wish it was you lying up there. I wish you were the one that had to go through that pain instead of my mum. You may not have killed her but you drove her to it!"

As Ross spat out his anger Billy reluctantly handed him a piece of paper, "it's from your mother," he said.

Ross read the suicide note from Maria and he felt guilt beginning to rush through his veins. "If I hadn't gone off to university none of this would have happened. You wouldn't have been able to hurt her the way you have!" He looked up from the note into his father's eyes and said in the calmest tone, "you're going to hell!"

Ross pushed his father back on to his chair and took his mobile phone out of his pocked and dialled 999. Ross expected Billy to run but he didn't, he sat there on the seat and waited to be carried away by the Police. He listened as he heard his son speak about him as though he was some kind of stranger who had come in from the street and carried out a random attack on a woman. Ross waited at the front door for the Police to arrive, all the while holding down the vomit that swam around his stomach.

My mum's dead, he thought as a single tear trickled down his cheek. *What am I going to do now?*

His mind was back in the present day. It would always be painful for Ross to relive that day but he sure as hell was not going to suffer it alone. Casually flicking through the paper and sipping at his coffee once more Ross knew that his life would never be complete, for it never had been.

He put his mug down and closed the newspaper. As he stood up, Rebecca's face looked up at him from the front page, as though she were looking deep into his eyes searching for an answer as to why he murdered her. He smiled at the picture, feeling no remorse for the young girl. He gave a sigh and walked over to the window which looked out onto the busy street, where to everyone else, life was normal. *Don't fret mum, by the time I am finished, there won't be any of them left.*

Five

One month after Maria's death

Ross was alone in Maria and Billy's home and wishing his mother to be alive and his father to be dead Ross began to feel his grief turn into sheer anger. At first he only blamed Billy but when he ran over it in his head again and again he realised that there were many people who played their part in Maria's death. What about the women, if you can even call them that? The women who all knew there was a wife, yet they still lay on their backs with the most repulsive human on the planet.

One month had passed since Maria had died, her funeral had come and gone, Billy had been arrested and put in prison, his plea of guilty to grievous bodily harm and rape prevented a trial and Ross from having to stand up in court and speak of his sordid childhood in front of a group of strangers.

The whole thing had suddenly come to a close and justice had been served – but to Ross, only in the eyes of the law was justice served. Ross had to clear out the house where he suffered as a child, hearing awful things and seeing things that a child should never have to see.

As he cleared out Maria's clothes and shoes, he raked through drawers and wardrobes, finding beautiful garments that smelled just like her. He smelled each item over and over, not wanting to forget his mothers scent. Each smell came with the memory of Maria's gentle face but immediately came the memory of torture. Ross came across a shoe box that was heavy and fit for bursting. He pulled it down from the top shelf of the wardrobe and carried it over to the bed. As he sat down he pulled the cardboard lid off and inside was numerous envelopes, all addressed to, "Son".

Ross felt a ripple of happiness pass through him as he saw the word on the envelopes. Had Maria left him something new to learn about her, something that only he and his mother would share without Billy having any control over it?

He opened the first envelope which sat at the top of the box, almost tearing the letter inside as he fumbled with it feeling excitement, curiosity and fear of what was inside.

Ross began to read, his heart pounding against the wall of his chest, his breathing short and fast. As he read, confusion began to set in;

1st April 1979

Son,

You may not know about me. I am your biological mother. I named you Jeffery Turner on the day you were born, however your name is likely to have been changed after you were adopted into your new family. This is my first letter to you since you went to your new family. I want you to know that my decision to give you away was not easy, in fact it was the hardest thing that I have ever had to do. I do not know what age you will be if you ever get to read this, so I do not know really how to tell you things. But all that you should know is that I would have been the best mum I would have known how to be and if I had had the chance I would have loved to see you grow. You should know that giving you up was the best thing for you, for reasons that you do not need to know right now. But the family that have taken you into their home will be able to give you the best life, a life that I am sad to say you could not have had with me. I sincerely hope that your life has been well lived so far and will continue to be great. I think of you every day and love you as much now as the day I gave birth to you. Maybe one day I could tell you that in person.

Love always

Maria Turner x

Ross stared down at the letter after he read it. He read it a few times, feeling the confusion turn to despair, "I have a brother?" he said aloud. He folded the letter and put it back into the envelope it was in, even though it was almost torn to shreds.

Ross emptied the box on to the bed and began to go through each envelope at a time, all of which were numbered one to four. There was a large envelope at the bottom of the box with Ross's name on it. Again he felt the anxiety take over at the realisation that Maria knew that he would find it one day and actually wanted to tell him about his older brother. His skin tingled, his forehead ached and his hands trembled as he opened the envelope labelled with his own name. Inside was a letter to him and an official form which read, 'Adoption Contact Scotland'.

Ross set the form aside and opened the letter;

Ross,

I understand that you must be feeling confused, maybe even angry. But please understand that I had to keep this from you for both our sakes. You know yourself that your father was a horrible man and if you knew about this then it would have made everything a million times worse. He made me do it Ross, I fought and fought but you know yourself fighting with Billy was like fighting a losing battle. Giving Jeffery away was the best thing for him. But then you came along six years later and I was not about to give you up. I fought for you and in the end I won. I kept you and I left him Ross. But in the end he clawed his way back in and it was the biggest mistake that I ever made. Because of that mistake you have had to endure so much and I am so sorry for putting you through that. You should have had the freedom I gave to Jeffery. I am sorry that I had to leave you and you had to find out that you have a brother this way but it was the only way to keep you safe. I know this must be horrible for you and I wish I could be there with you when you find this but please know that no matter what I always loved you and I wish that things could have been different. I have put you through so much and I thought that the least I could do was give you the opportunity to find the last remaining part of me. I am not saying that you have to but the opportunity is there if you want to take it, even if it is in years to come. All you have to do is fill in the form and send it off and the adoption people will do the rest. I hope that you can gain some happiness in life and put all of our horrible past behind you.

I love you Ross, always remember that, Mum x.

Ross hadn't realised it but he had cried his way through the letter. They were tears of rage. Rage towards Billy for making Maria give away her first baby, rage that he had been kept in the dark for so long about his brother. But mainly, Ross was angry for himself, he had been given the short straw. Why did he have to suffer Billy as a dad, this Jeffery character had been given a, 'get out of jail free card,' and Ross was beginning to feel cheated.

"None of this is your fault Mum," he said aloud. "None of it."

Ross carried on clearing out the house for the rest of the day, all the while thinking of everything that had happened in the last twenty odd years, he was thinking of Jeffery.

He finally finished clearing the house and as he made his way home in a taxi, he carried with him the box that contained a new world of information, that Ross wasn't quite sure how to cope with.

Six

1st December 2007- Collection time 7:30am

He watched the Royal Mail van approaching the post box as he clutched at the envelope in his hands. It was just coming on seven thirty in the morning and Ross had been standing next to the post box for the past twenty minutes. It was still pitch black outside and he watched the freezing fog hover underneath the street lamps.

He wanted to personally hand the envelope to the postman to make sure that it didn't get lost as he emptied the post in to the large post sack. It was freezing and the snow that lay on the ground had frozen too. Ross didn't feel the cold on this morning. There was too much going on to bother about the temperature.

The van pulled up beside him and the driver got out. He stopped and looked at Ross, who was still clutching at his envelope.

"Are you going to post that sir?" he asked Ross.

This is it, the moment that could change everything that has gone wrong, he thought to himself.

"Sir, did you hear me?"

"Yes I am, but could you just put it straight into that sack. I want to see you take it away, I need to see it being carried off in that van, if it's not too much to ask?" Ross looked on at the man, who was already reaching over to take the envelope from him.

"Whatever mate, I just want to get back into my van, its bloody freezing out here. You should put a jacket on before you catch your death!" the driver said as he unlocked the post box and began hauling the post into the sack.

It won't be me catching my death sir, Ross thought, "Thanks mate, appreciate it."

Ross crossed the road and made his way back up the stairs and continued on his train of thought.

He couldn't believe how easy it was and how good it made him feel. He never used to think that revenge could make things better but for the first time in six months, Ross felt less grief stricken than he ever had. His thoughts referred to the murder that he had committed the evening before. A young homeless woman he had stumbled across in the street had begged him for money after he had already said no.

"Please, I need the money for food and it is so cold out here. Can't you spare anything?" she had asked again, this time a little more aggressively.

Ross could feel his patience running out.

As she looked at him with eyes of hunger and anger, Ross felt the fuse burn out inside him. "Follow me and I will give you what I have in my pocket, I don't want any of your homeless friends seeing this or they will pounce on me," he said.

He led her along the street and turned down an alley way that ran parallel to a main road. The alley was the access point to the large dustbins for the restaurants and takeaways that were situated there. The woman had no reservations about following him, none at all.

She was so desperate for money that she couldn't risk him changing his mind, so she made the quick decision that mugging him was her safest bet. Just as she was about to make her move, he stopped suddenly in front of her and turned to face her. She had moved up so closely behind him that when he did turn around, there noses were almost touching.

"Oh, you're keen," he said with a smile.

She suddenly felt doubt in her mind and realised that she was alone with a strange man in an alleyway. It was pitch dark and the alley was not lit.

"I am just starving," she tried to hide the doubt in her voice.

"Must be horrible living out here, especially at Christmas time?" Ross was good at putting sympathy into his tone.

"You get used to it," she said, beginning to lose her nerve.

"Why don't I put you out of your misery?" Ross smiled and put his hand into his pocket.

As the woman watched his hand move to his pocket, she felt a little more at ease and she let out a silent sigh of relief and dropped her chin to her chest.

Ross watched her do so and as she lifted her head back up to face him, she was shocked to feel his fist meet her jaw. She fell to the ground and as she struggled to get back up and run from him, he was suddenly on top of her with his cold hands around her throat.

He was heavy and extremely strong. She was no match for him. She couldn't scream, couldn't move. All she knew was that she was going to die.

He closed the door of his flat and made his way into the bedroom. As he lay in bed looking up at the ceiling, he replayed in his head the look on her face as he killed her.

When he heard her last breath squeeze out of her mouth, he felt the release of a weight, like some grief went with the dead girl's soul. Leaving her in the dustbin outside the back of the restaurant was the hardest part, not for his conscience, no not for that. It was the physical work of it that was the hardest part. She was literally a dead weight. But he had managed it and with great pleasure too.

"Homeless people are easy targets," he told her lifeless body as it lay inside the bin. "No-one will miss you!"

And no one did, it wasn't on the news and there were no missing person's adverts in the papers or shop windows. He was right, no one missed her.

Homeless girls weren't the ones he wanted though, he wanted the ones who caused him and his mother the most pain. That was the type of satisfaction he was looking for and if it was out there then he was going to take it! He needed a challenge, needed to set himself some targets, but how?

"Let's see what I can do next," he said to himself as he fell asleep.

Seven

Death's prophecy

Early on the morning of the 1st August 2010, Patrick sat at the breakfast bar in his city centre flat reading the headlines of, 'The Record,' in disbelief. 'Third female found dead in city.'

He couldn't quite get his thoughts straight, he couldn't even tell if they were his own thoughts at this time. He had been having very strong visions and voices running through his head in recent weeks. They were so graphic and clear that sometimes he had to remind himself that he wasn't having a conversation with a live human being!

He sipped at his steaming hot coffee, the first of many that morning and he read on;

A young woman has been found dead in the city centre in the early hours of this morning. The young woman, who has not yet been named, was found in an alley just off St Vincent Square by a cleaner who was disposing of rubbish from one of the local pubs that she works in.

She is the third female to have been found dead in the city in the last two months. A post mortem has yet to be carried out but it is likely that she is the latest victim of the recent murders to have taken place in Glasgow's city centre.

In link with the two current cases Strathclyde Police have confirmed that they are running voluntary DNA sample checks at Pitt Street station.

White males between the ages of 20 and 30 years old who were in the city centre at the times of these horrendous murders are invited to give voluntary DNA samples to help with their enquiries.

Patrick's reading was interrupted when his fiancée Jodie put her hand on his shoulder.

He took another sip of coffee and turned to her. "Morning" he said.

Jodie looked at the newspaper on the breakfast bar and sighed. "Another one?" she asked, knowing his response.

"Looks like it!" said Patrick keeping his eyes on Jodie.

"When did it happen?" Jodie asked.

"Just last night going by what the paper is saying."

Jodie and Patrick had been together forever, ever since that first meeting at school all those years ago. They were soul mates and had so much understanding between them. Jodie was aware that Patrick had had some trouble sleeping over the last few weeks, ever since the first killing had been reported. She knew exactly why, but never mentioned it directly to him. She didn't want to invade his thoughts anymore than they already were. She could see that he had taken his eyes off of her and had moved them back to the newspaper report he had been reading when she had first entered their medium sized kitchen.

Patrick and Jodie had been living together since they were just nineteen years old. Patrick's parents, Derek and Sue were killed in a horrific car accident just before his 19th birthday and their death almost killed Patrick. He had been so close to them and his Grandparents who had passed away when Patrick was very young. Not a lot of people can say that they are close to their Grandparents at a very young age but Patrick could. He and his Grandpa especially, after all they did share a special gift. Patrick's gift could allow contact with any spirit however he could never make contact with Derek and Sue. His Grandpa would say that their spirits left their human forms so quickly because of impact that they could have been in shock and that was perhaps the reason that Patrick couldn't contact them.

Jodie's heart ached for Patrick when Derek and Sue were killed, all she wanted to do was comfort him but no amount of comfort would change the loss of his parents.

After Derek and Sue's deaths, Patrick moved in with Jodie at her parent's house and they saved money to buy their own place.

Six years later they moved in to their flat in Glasgow harbour. It was at that point that Patrick began to feel happy again, he finally felt like he had something to live for.

As they began their new life together they also began running the new West End Spiritualist Church, Patrick took this upon himself at first mainly because of his parent's death. He wanted to help others who had lost someone close to them and give some sort of comfort. Their friends and family knew that they were spiritually gifted and to begin with, Jodie's parent's were not entirely happy with the idea but in the end they came to understand it. Life was going well for them, both having successful jobs and a successful church. However, recent weeks were proving difficult for Patrick and he was beginning to lose control over his ability. He was receiving messages so often that he was losing sleep and as the weeks had gone on and the news reported now of a third murder, Patrick was beginning to figure things out slowly.

Jodie stood behind him whilst he read the report. She wrapped her arms around him and kissed him on the back of the neck. She felt him relax a little under her embrace.

"You're tired aren't you?" she asked, but it was almost like she was stating a fact.

"You have no idea how exhausted I feel Jodie. My mind has been vividly awake for the past eight weeks. Whilst my body feels rested, my mind feels like it has been actively awake the entire time. I feel like someone is watching me, entering my thoughts. There is no space for my own thinking and I'm having visions that do not belong in my head," he sounded tormented.

She felt it. She knew what it felt like to have a bombardment of voices in her head during the night. The only difference being that Jodie's 'memories' were just voices. Some lost spirit who had stumbled across her and just wanted to put something into her head, nothing serious or sinister, just a memory of grandchildren or a favourite song. There were no visions with Jodie.

Patrick's senses on the other hand were a little different. He had visions, other people's visions, past lives and memories. Most of which were not very pleasant. Some spirits would project visual memories of abuse within a family, alcohol related illnesses which led to death, stresses of life which led to suicide. His visions were constant, but over the years he was able to block out some of them at times when he wanted his thoughts to be his own.

But over the last eight weeks or so, Patrick had found it exceptionally hard to block out his visions.

He turned in the bar stool which he was sat on and looked at Jodie. She knew he was going to tell all by the look on his face but she didn't know to what extent.

"It's all been remarkably clear, especially at night. When you have been asleep next to me at night, I have felt like someone else. Like I don't know who you are..." he stared at her, in disarray at his own words.

"What do you mean? Like you don't *know me* anymore?" Jodie asked, also baffled.

"No, not like that, it's like *I* am someone else Jodie. The visions and memories at night have taken control over my own mind that I feel like I am the person who is trying to contact me. The only thing is this time it's different." He looked back at the newspaper report and lifted his coffee. He sipped at it again, only to find it had gone cold.

"It's not just one person is it?" Jodie understood immediately at that point what Patrick was trying to tell her.

"I have been trying to piece together the visions and memories that are being put into my head and I think I have finally finished the puzzle," he said almost excited now.

He looked back up from the newspaper and put his hands on Jodie's shoulders, as if to steady her for what was about to come.

"Last night you saw the mess I was in, talking about that woman in the sitting room. What I saw was horrible, she looked like she had been dragged along the ground on a wet night, her clothing was covered in what seemed like oil, dirt from the ground and her hair looked like a wig in bad need of a wash, which had been put on backwards." Jodie almost laughed at the wig comment. It was as if he was trying to make light of what had happened, what was happening.

"But that is not the only time I have experienced her, well her for the first time yes, but I've been having visions of two others too, same kind of state, dirty clothes, bruising and just a complete mess. You've missed me seeing all of this because you have been in bed while I'm pacing the flat, desperate for sleep."

He was nodding now, as if everything had just been pieced together. "Jodie I think the spirits who are trying to contact me are the three women who have just been murdered."

Eight

Patrick's purpose

Jodie stood in the shower. She needed some alone time to process the conversation she had just had with her fiancée. Not that it was brand new information to her that he was able to communicate with the dead, to put it bluntly, obviously she was able to do that too. But she had never seen him so affected by it before now.

The hot water powered down on her neck and back and trickled down her face as she stood there, wondering what would come of the visions Patrick had been having. She thought about all of the sleepless nights he had been having and how tired he had been over the last eight weeks or so.

She finished bathing herself and climbed out of the shower. She walked into the bedroom that she shared with Patrick and sat on the bed with the towel wrapped around her. Patrick entered the room and sat next to Jodie. There was silence for a while.

"The Police are asking that any white males aged between twenty and thirty who were in the city centre the nights of the murders should go to give a voluntary DNA sample." He looked at Jodie as she sat on the edge of the bed listening.

"Have they found traces of DNA on the women?" Jodie asked.

"Apparently so. We were in town the night the first girl was murdered, so I'm going to give a sample." He expected protest. It would be just like her.

"Well if you think it will help," she took his hand in a reassuring manner. "It may put your mind at rest too," she hoped.

"I think I can help. I have had visions of these women in not so pleasant circumstances and I don't even know them Jodie, never met them before in my life! I think I could really help their investigations," he said with sincerity in his voice.

Jodie looked at him and in her head she knew exactly what he meant.

"Wait a minute Patrick, if you go wading in there giving information that the police will see as only the murderer could know they're going to start asking questions as to why you know so much and in so much detail. Please remember that not all people in the world believe in what we do." She was squeezing his hand as she spoke.

Patrick considered this for a moment. He thought to himself that she could be right, but the DNA sample would prove to the police that he had nothing to do with the murders.

"You think that they are going to believe you the minute you tell the Police what you've seen? I understand it but there is a real chance that they won't. Think about it Patrick, really think about it. You will be putting yourself at risk of becoming a suspect," she pleaded.

Patrick didn't say anything, he just stared at her. But he was far away. He thought about the most recent girl to be murdered. He didn't have her name yet as she was thrown into death so suddenly that it hadn't been made known to him. He referred to her as the third girl. He took his thoughts back to the night of the first murder.

He and Jodie had been in town that night for a meal. They had walked home from Bath Street to the harbour where they live. It was a summer's night and it was turning darker as they walked.

They could have passed the murderer. It could have been Jodie that was murdered. Who would be their next victim? That's why he felt the need to help the Police. But how could he get them to believe him, or even understand? He thought about the crushing sensation he had felt during the early hours of the first time he encountered the spirit of the first murdered woman. He had fallen asleep, but it was a restless sleep. He had been dreaming of a woman who didn't have a face, kind of like a video clip and the editor had put a blur on the characters face. She was running. Patrick ran along side her in the dream, but he had no clue as to who she was. She was young, perhaps in her early twenties with long dark hair, it was damp and hung around the sides of her face as she ran. Her long side fringe was damp and flopping over her face as she ran. Patrick had a fear in him he couldn't comprehend. He felt terror in his veins, and his heart thumped so hard in his chest that he honestly thought it would burst through his chest at any moment. He watched the girl who ran, in bare feet he noticed. She kept looking behind her, which made Patrick look behind him too. He understood there and then what the girl was running from. The black silhouette of a man wasn't far behind them and he was also running.

Patrick's head began to thump. He ached from the top of his spine to the bottom. He suddenly felt himself willing this girl to run faster. He felt the presence of the silhouette behind them and all of a sudden he felt like he was being sucked up into the air. He watched as the silhouette jumped on top of the girl and pushed her face hard into the ground. Patrick himself felt the weight of the man as if he had jumped on top of him. He watched helplessly as the girl struggled for her life. The man who had been pursuing her was now strangling her.

Patrick was beginning to have what felt like a panic attack, but in fact he was feeling what the girl was feeling, he was suffocating. The silhouette had wrapped his fingers around her throat and squeezed, digging his fingernails into her skin so hard that he drew blood. Patrick squeezed his eyes shut, he couldn't bare to watch the horrible nightmare he was caught in! As he squeezed his eyes shut he could hear the girl choking on the man's grip, gasping for air to fill her lungs. He opened them and saw the girl was looking up at him, still faceless. She reached out for him as he looked down on the horror she faced. He felt his stomach lurch, and suddenly he sat bolt upright in bed and was gasping for breath!

He immediately felt relief from the nightmare he had been in. He turned the bedside lamp on and he felt that awful surge of fear again as he saw the girls face in the corner of the room. She didn't say anything, she just reached out for him, making the same gasping motions as he had when he watched her in the nightmare. He stared at her, wondering who she was, what she wanted. He had used his ability to try to communicate with her. He spoke softly in his head to her, using a calmness that was hard to surface in the situation he faced.

"Who are you? What do you need?"

She was showing him in the only way that she could that she had suffocated. The only way she could show him was to go into his mind and replay the events leading up to her death.

But why? Why had this young life been taken so brutally?

Now, weeks after his first vision there were three spirits in his head and he knew that there was no way he would get any sleep unless he did something to help.

"Jodie, I have to try, this isn't just about us now. I can't keep this in just so we don't get scrutinised for something that some people don't believe in. Times have changed since we were kids Jodie. People aren't as afraid of the spirit world as they used to be, people are more curious now and much more open minded. Look at all those states in America where the Police use psychic and spiritualist mediums to help in murder investigations. And in so many of the cases the mediums have been almost one hundred percent accurate in their evidence!" She took his other hand and pulled him round to face her.

"Tell me exactly what you have seen," she looked deep into his eyes and held his hands tight.

Patrick closed his eyes and relaxed his thoughts. He thought about the things he had seen over the last eight weeks. He shuddered at how cruel and callous this man was. He thought about all of the many reasons that he could be using to excuse why he had killed these women. Patrick tried so desperately to put a face to the shadow he saw chasing the woman in his dream. But the harder he tried the more distant the dream became. He thought about the place he had been taken too in his dream and how he felt when he was there. He could feel the terror pulsing through his body.

The spirit of that woman was trying so desperately to make Patrick feel and understand how scared she had felt. He understood from that moment of realisation what exactly was happening. He knew then what he had to do! He had no face for this man. But he would do all he could to find it. Three innocent lives had come to a complete end and Patrick's thoughts were how many more before the callous, heartless excuse for a human could be stopped?

Patrick opened his eyes said, "The women who have been in my dreams and appearing in front of me almost every night..."

Jodie nodded, as if she was already expecting what he was about to say.

"They have been showing me exactly what happened to them. They want me to help find the person who murdered them."

Nine

Revelations of Dreams

Patrick stepped out of the shower, dried himself and went straight to the bedroom to put on his clothes. He picked up a t-shirt and jeans from the wardrobe and practically threw them on.

"Why are you in such a hurry Patrick? It's not as if your DNA is going to help. It's only going to narrow the search down by one person!" Jodie said.

"It's not about the DNA Jodie, it's about what I have to say. What I can do to help them." Patrick was sitting at the edge of the bed now putting on his socks and a pair of Nike trainers. He stood up and kissed Jodie on the cheek as he passed her on the way out of the bedroom door.

"You're going now?"

"No time like the present. I'll not be long."

"Wait! Why don't I come with you?" Jodie asked. She was thinking that this was not the best idea and the Police were just going to laugh in his face.

"Really? Why do you want to come?" Patrick knitted his eyebrows in curiosity.

"For support when the Police tell you that you are wasting their time!" Jodie tried to sound as empathetic as possible. "I understand why you are doing this Patrick because I know what your goal is. But do you honestly think that they are going to have time to sit and listen to someone that they are going to see as telling ghost stories?"

"You don't think they'll hear what I have to say?" Patrick sounded annoyed.

"I think that they will listen, but I also think that this could go two ways for you. They will either have no interest in your story or, they will and wonder why the hell you have so much information."

Patrick considered this for a moment. Jodie had stopped him in his tracks, like she had always managed to do. Whether she emerged from the bedroom wearing her finest dress or first thing in the morning with bed head, she always managed to make him stop, just for a second. She had always had such an influence over him no matter what the situation. He loved that about her, but he also despised it! He closed his eyes for just a second and when he opened them the murdered women were in his line of sight, stood behind Jodie at the window. This time looking as normal as he and Jodie were at that particular moment. Then they were gone again in the blink of an eye. It was as if they were reminding him of what he had been shown.

Patrick had remained calm throughout and seeing their faces helped him make his decision, "I'm doing this. If you are coming I'm leaving now!" Patrick went in to the kitchen to get his wallet and went to the front door.

Jodie was stood there waiting, "Just be careful of the way you word things ok? I just don't like the thought of you..."

Patrick put his index finger over her mouth and smiled. "No need to be worrying about me Jodie, if anything, I should be worrying about you. There's a crazy killer on the loose out there and he is targeting young women."

Jodie shuddered at the thought and went into the hall to get her handbag, "Well if you put it like that then I am definitely coming with you!" she smiled, but inside for the first time she felt a genuine discomfort about the murder reports.

She, for the first time sensed something bad was coming, but couldn't quite pin point what it was, most likely another senseless death.

As Patrick and Jodie descended the stairs of the modern style apartments overlooking the west end and south side of Glasgow,

Jodie noticed how the sun shone strongly through the landing windows. It made her think of the beautiful sunrises that those three women would never get to see again. She realised then why it was so important for Patrick to give his information to the Police. This monster couldn't get away with what he had done to these women.

What if this person had planned more killings? What if this was just the start? Patrick interrupted her thoughts. "Should we just walk? It's nice weather for walking, not too hot."

He looked at Jodie, waiting for a response that didn't come. He gently placed a hand upon her shoulder. "Jodie? Are you ok?"

"Yeah, let's walk," she said. "Sorry, I was miles away."

They exited the secure door entry system and crossed the not so busy road of South Street and began to walk through the underpass of the express way which their apartment faced. Jodie slipped her hand into Patricks grip. "So, what exactly are you going to say to the Police when we get there?" Jodie asked with curiosity.

"I don't really know yet to be honest. I'll just say what comes to mind. I'll probably just tell them what I told you. That I've been seeing things that resemble the stories in the news and just see what happens from there."

They came out from the underpass onto Dumbarton road where cars were a constant hum along each side of the road and the buzz of conversations spoken by the hundreds of people that bustled along the pavement was deafening. Jodie looked around at the mix of different cultures that surrounded her.

"It could be anyone Patrick. We could be standing right next to him right now and have no clue. Those three women wouldn't have had a clue either!" She tightened the grip on Patrick's hand.

He turned to look at her as they weaved in and out of the busy people on the street and said, "It will be alright you know. The Police will catch him with or without my help."

"I hope you are right Patrick, I just have a really bad feeling about it all."

Both of them stopped talking as they made their way through the manic shoppers that hurried their way along the street. The scent in the air was typical of a Glasgow day, traffic fumes and cigarette smoke. They made their way through the hustle and bustle for about ten minutes before coming to the Glasgow art gallery and museum, where the pavement harboured less people and Jodie felt like she could finally exhale.

They continued to walk toward the city centre where the Police station was situated, talking about their situation as they did. They could feel a gentle, warm summer breeze on their faces as they walked and there was a beer garden on the other side of the street, filled with people laughing and talking as they enjoyed the sun shining down on them, something that occurred on a rare occasion in Glasgow.

Jodie looked over and wished that for that moment, she could be sitting in that beer garden, not worrying about Patrick and not having the knot in her stomach that she couldn't explain. "Do you think it will be busy when we get there?" asked Jodie.

"Of people giving DNA samples? I don't know, can't say I have ever given one before, so I don't know what to expect," Patrick squeezed Jodie's hand tight as they climbed the four steps at the entrance of Pitt Street Police station.

It was a long sand coloured building with large mirror reflection windows up the left side of the building. Patrick opened the door that had the Strathclyde Police logo across the middle of the glass panel and let Jodie go inside first. The reception area was quite big with blue plastic seats all along the left hand side which were all empty. On the right hand side was a large plastic wall rack with lots of information leaflets and posters. The reception desk was at the back of the room and there were two uniformed officers standing behind it, one was filling out paper work and the other was on the phone.

"Now that I think of it, I was expecting it to be slightly busier than this," said Patrick as they both approached the desk.

The officer who was filling out paperwork looked up from his papers and smiled at both Jodie and Patrick. "What can I do for you?"

"My name is Patrick McLaughlin and I am here with some information on the city centre murder inquiries and to give a voluntary DNA sample," he almost held his breath after he spoke.

"Ok I just need to take a few details and I can get someone to speak with you."

Patrick filled out the paperwork that was necessary and was asked to wait in the seating area whilst the officer fetched someone to come and speak to him.

He could feel a build up of nerves in the middle of his stomach, under the breastbone. It was a feeling of butterflies and heartburn combined.

"Are you ok babe? You've gone really pale!" said Jodie who was sitting to the left of him.

"I all of a sudden feel really nervous but I've got nothing to feel nervous about," his voice was almost shaking.

"Of course you are feeling nervous Patrick, you are about to tell the Police that you have seen three women being murdered but you weren't actually there!" Patrick thought of this and realised that she was right, but knew he couldn't go back, he had to speak to the Police. The visions would only get worse.

"Patrick McLaughlin? D.S Preston will see you now, I'll take you through," said the officer.

"I'll wait here," Jodie gave a reassuring smile as Patrick stood up.

The officer led Patrick down a short corridor and into a room that you would normally see in programmes like 'Law and Order

UK' or 'The Bill'. It had a small table with four chairs around it and a small window in the back wall. The room had been painted a cold blue colour and it was obvious to Patrick that it was not of recent decor. The paint had bubbled and chipped all around the top where the walls met the ceiling and the window was covered in dust. D.S Preston entered the room with his colleague D.C Lang.

D.S Preston motioned for Patrick to take a seat at the far side of the table. He did and the two Detectives sat opposite him. D.S Preston was a tall man about five feet nine, who had been on the job for about twenty five years. His face was worn and tired looking but his mannerisms definitely weren't. He seemed like the happy sort that would get on great with everyone, but Patrick figured he was also the type he wouldn't want to get on the wrong side of.

D.C Lang was about the same height with a receding hairline and a beer belly. Both officers were holding polystyrene cups filled with milky coffees from the vending machine in the corridor.

"Have a seat," D.C Lang gestured with his hand to the opposite side of the table from the door.

"So, Mr McLaughlin, I understand that you have some information for us regarding the murders of Rebecca Collins, Michelle Levine and Angela Noble?" asked D.S Preston. He had a strong Scottish accent, which made his voice sound loud and rather intimidating.

So that's her name, Patrick thought to himself. He proceeded to speak. "Yes, but you may find my information a little far fetched." His mouth began to dry up as spoke to the two men across the table.

This is going to sound crazy, he thought to himself again but he certainly was not about to stop.

"What do you mean, far fetched Mr McLaughlin?" D.C Lang knitted his eyebrows and took a sip of coffee.

"Let me finish my whole story before you comment on it please?" he asked.

Both officers looked at each other then back to Patrick. D.S Preston said, "Ok, go ahead Mr McLaughlin."

D.S Preston stayed upright in his chair and D.C Lang sat back on the chairs back support. Patrick began his version of the recent events, just hoping that the police were as open minded and believing as he and Jodie were. He had more hope in Preston than in Lang. Preston came across to Patrick as open minded, and it's not like mediums have never worked alongside the police before. Lang, on the other hand seemed like his mind was somewhere else, lunch probably.

Patrick had his fingers crossed under the table the whole time, after all, justice depended on it.

Ten

Believer or Sceptic

D.S Preston sat on the edge of the table after three hours in the interview room with Patrick and his partner D.C Lang. Patrick had just given a swab from the inside of his mouth. He had also just finished explaining everything that he had experienced.

"OK I think we could all do with some coffee," said D.S Preston standing up and taking a stretch. He motioned D.C Lang to the door.

"We'll be back in a tick, coffee Mr McLaughlin?" asked D.C Lang.

"Yeah, great thanks," Patrick answered distantly.

D.S Preston closed the door behind them and the colleagues began walking down the corridor towards the vending machine.

"So... he's crackers eh?" D.C Lang suggested with a big sarcastic grin on his face.

"Jim, you never were the understanding type were you?" Preston put his money in the machine and pressed the button for strong black coffee.

"Come on now Paul you're not seriously suggesting that this guy is of the sane mind, are you? He is one hundred percent involved in this case. There's no way he could have known all of those things about the individual murders if he wasn't!" Lang protested.

"Well the DNA will prove any physical involvement at least, anything else after that will just have to wait until the results arrive. We will specifically request a quick result for Mr McLaughlin's DNA." Preston gave Lang two coffees and pressed the button for one more.

Paul Preston and Jim Lang had been partners for ten years or so. They had worked together on many cases, all of which had been solved through hard work, determination and a large pint of lager at the end of each shift, to say the least. They had become best friends over the years after spending so many late night shifts and interrogations together. They were good men, a good laugh at times, and they loved their families dearly. But they did live their days with their heads in the job. It was the best job anyone could ask for, catching petty and proper, fearful criminals and working their backsides off to put them away for a very long time. If it was up to Preston and Lang there would be no time limit at all for the likes of murderers, rapists and paedophiles.

"Put them all on a desert island in the middle of the sea miles away from land and innocent human life and let them fight amongst themselves. That's my motto!" Preston would always say.

Both Preston and Lang had grown up children in their twenties. Preston in particular had a daughter at twenty something years old and so this particular case was hitting a raw nerve, considering the circumstances.

"Aye, maybe you're right Paul, but I'm not so sure. There's something dodgy about this McLaughlin lad. He knows too much not to be involved!" Lang went on as Preston retrieved the third coffee from the machine.

They walked back along the corridor towards the interview room where they had left Patrick.

"Jim, don't be so negative about him just yet. In my years of cases like this, the murderer doesn't just pop up out of nowhere with graphic details the way Patrick has. He knows what has happened to these victims in graphic detail yes, but how? I'll hold my hands up if the DNA comes back matching that of the sample taken from the girls, fair enough. I've got a feeling that he is telling us the truth!" Preston kept his head facing the direction they were headed down the corridor.

Lang stopped dead on his feet and laughed in disbelief. "Are you bloody serious Paul? There's no way you're serious," Lang was beginning to sound slightly annoyed.

"Well unless he is the pathologist that carried out the post mortems, which we both know he isn't then I'm willing to hear him out a little more!" Preston smiled sarcastically at Lang then he motioned to the door. "Shall we?"

Preston opened the door and held it open for Lang since he was carrying two cups of hot coffee. Lang handed a cup to Patrick who smiled briefly at him. Preston closed the door behind Lang and both officers sat down opposite Patrick.

"You both think I'm mad don't you?" asked Patrick.

"Well, I myself am slightly more intrigued by your revelations than D.C Lang here, but what I would like to know is how you, Mr McLaughlin feel you can help us in this case like you said at the beginning?" Preston asked seriously.

"Well, whether you believe me or not or whether or not you believe in the afterlife, this is real for me...as real as it gets actually. So what I'm saying here is that I can help your investigation by leading you to the murderer of these girls." Patrick was shaking with nerves inside but his physical presence was that of a man who was confident in his words.

D.C Lang couldn't take his eyes off Patrick as he spoke. He was the biggest sceptic out there, but even he felt like Patrick's words were sounding confident.

"So, how can you lead us to the murderer exactly?" Lang tried not to sound unprofessional. "No offence kid, but your story doesn't seem like something solid that we can use to put to our superior to work with here!"

Preston kept facing Patrick's direction but his eyes rolled towards Lang as he spoke. This was the first time in twenty odd years that the two colleagues were in a slight disagreement.

"I can completely understand your scepticism concerning this particular situation Sir, but I am a man of my word. What I do is completely, one hundred percent legitimate. The spirits of the victims have shown me the individual places they each took their last breath, the clothing they were wearing, the injuries they had, even the drinks they had on the night that they were killed. I am not looking for any credit for myself here, all I want is a clear head, and to know that my fiancée will feel safe, out at night again."

Patrick sat back on his chair and ran his hands over his scalp, looking on at Preston and Lang. He had never met any of these women before in his life, in this case only in their death. He knew nothing about them or their families. He knew nothing about anything to do with them, yet it seemed now more than before, he wanted to catch this sick minded killer and help put him away for a very long time.

Preston stood up and put his hands on the back of Lang's chair, who then also proceeded to stand up and walked to the back of the room.

"Mr McLaughlin, the DNA results will be with us in a few days, you'll be hearing from us with regards to that if there are any developments." Preston said with a slight smile.

"Alright, thank you for your time." Patrick got up and Lang opened the door for him.

Once the door was closed and Patrick was on the other side, there was silence for a few moments.

Lang approached the table again and standing behind Preston he said, "You believe every word he has just said, don't you?"

"Well, we don't seem to have any other damn leads in this investigation do we? The murderer is a bloody professional by the looks of it. Either that or he is invisible. There is not a single trace of him!" Preston said.

"Well remember we are still waiting on DNA." Lang nodded his head, "I know what you're going to say and yes I'm thinking it too!"

"I'm thinking that any murderer in their sane mind, if any, wouldn't give a voluntary DNA sample." Preston confirmed Lang's expectation.

Eleven

Mark

The Blue Bar was absolutely heaving on Friday evening, people were ordering food and cocktails and you could hear a thousand conversations going on around all the tables and bar sides. The bar itself was in the middle of the room with five staff working behind it. Its decor was very classy, with a spiral staircase at the back leading to a seated area where black leather couches and seats darted around the place. Around the top of the bar were lots of blue LED lights which highlighted all of the bottles of spirits and glasses. Staff stood behind the bar making cocktails. The sound of alcohol being shaken in with the ice and the smell of fancy foods being cooked from scratch by the wonderfully talented chefs was relaxing to the customers and the norm to staff.

The Blue Bar had a reputation of class, sophistication and never a dull night was to be had. That's why Patrick loved working there so much. He had worked in the bar for two years and it got better each night he was there. For some reason though, tonight was stressful. A member of bar staff recently left and hadn't been replaced so everything was a big rush.

As Patrick took a fifteen minute break, he decided to go out to the back for a cigarette. He walked down the stairs to go out to the back door when the manager's office door opened.

"Ah Patrick, just who I was looking for," said William, the manager of The Blue Bar.

"Oh? What I have I done now?" Patrick laughed taking out his cigarettes.

"Nothing at all, can I borrow you for one moment though?" William asked sounding excited. William was an over excited, enthusiastic about everything type of man. Patrick liked this about

65

him. It helped keep him upbeat about things too, especially on nights like tonight when service was rushed.

"Sure can, but I only have fifteen so make it quick Willie."

Patrick had become very friendly with William over the last two years whilst working in the bar. Patrick wasn't the assistant to William, but if ever there were a problem within work, William would always call on him.

Patrick went inside the office and he noticed that William had a visitor with him.

"Hi," said the third man whom Patrick did not recognise.

"Patrick this is Mark, Mark - Patrick!" William said introducing them.

Mark was tall, with dark hair gelled back from his face. His skin was quite tanned and he was smartly dressed in a white shirt, black trousers and a black tie.

"Mark is our new member of the bar staff. He will be starting his shifts tonight and I really wanted you to be the one to show him the ropes?" William suggested to Patrick.

"No bother at all. So have you worked in bars before Mark?" Patrick shook his hand.

"Here and there when I was at University, you been here long?"

"Two years, so I'll be able to show you everything there is to know about the bar upstairs. But before I do I really need this smoke. Do you fancy one before we start the night?" Patrick held the pack out to Mark.

"Yeah that would be good, but I have my own thanks!" Mark took a pack out of his back pocket and both men proceeded to move towards the office door.

Even though it was the summer time, there was a slight chill in the air when the breeze caught their skin.

"So what's your story? Have you always lived in Glasgow?" Patrick asked as he lit his cigarette.

"I've lived all over really. Lived down in Bristol for a while when I was a Uni, then I moved back up here around two years ago when I finished studying," Mark replied, dragging on his cigarette in between his words, "what about you?"

"Yep, always been a Glasgow man, wouldn't leave this place even if I wanted to. I live with my fiancée down at Glasgow harbour."

"Nice. Bet they're expensive to rent?" Mark dropped the cigarette on the ground and crushed it with his shoe and continued, "Sorry that sounded really nosy!"

"A lot of people say that to me when I tell them where I live. To be honest they are really expensive but we bought it so it's cheaper than it would be to rent it." Patrick put out the cigarette and held the door open for Mark to go inside first.

As they ascended the stairs the music from the bar above sounded far away and the sounds that were heard were the base and beat of the music and the echoing conversations being had by the people being wined and dined by the staff left to run the bar.

"It gets really busy on Friday nights in here so we probably won't get a chance to talk till closing. But I will show you the basics and anything else we can deal with if it crops up, does that sound ok?" Patrick asked as they reached the door leading into the bar.

"Sounds like a plan!"

As they entered the bustling room, Patrick led Mark behind the bar and showed him where everything was kept and how to run the till. The night progressed well, with plenty of cash being exchanged across the bar and food service was running at a good pace. One well dressed woman approached the bar with a piece of white card in her hand. She was waiting a few moments whilst Mark served a customer before her.

"What can I get for you?" Mark asked politely.

The woman wore a sleek knee length dress which fitted her figure perfectly, with slim straps. Her hair hung in loose dark blond curls around her face and her lips were shimmering under the lights.

"My drinks list is on this, I'd never remember it otherwise!" she smiled.

Mark took the card from her and began making his way through the list. He had his back to the woman as he made up the drinks when Patrick came to his side and said, "Think she has a thing for you!"

"Who?" Mark tried to play dumb, but he knew fine well she was watching him. He could feel her eyes on the back of his neck.

"The lady in the black dress, and if I'm not mistaken, isn't that a name and phone number on the back there?" Patrick took the card from the counter where Mark had placed it and flipped it over.

"How'd you manage to notice that?" Mark was laughing now.

"I saw it on the back when she handed you the card. Think you've got yourself a lady for the night my friend," Patrick imitated a Sean Connery accent with a sarcastic grin on his face.

"We shall see. I'm not one to date the customers," Mark continued to make the drinks.

"Are you serious?"

"No. Look at her," Mark laughed. Finishing the last drink he winked at Patrick as he turned to his admirer.

"Here we are, that will be fifteen pounds and ninety pence please." Mark placed the drinks down in front of the woman and looked straight into her eyes. As she handed him the money he gently clasped his hand around her and said, "What is your name?"

She almost crumbled under the electricity that ran up her arm the minute he touched her. She kept her composure and answered in a steady voice, "Anna."

"Lovely, Anna. I'm Mark and I am going to be making use of this little card that you gave me. How's about I give you a call tonight and we can arrange a date?"

"Ok that sounds great," she smiled widely, collected her drinks and went back to the table where her friends were waiting.

Patrick looked on in amazement. He felt like he were in the middle of a fifties romance movie.

"That was something else, she was like putty in your hands." Patrick put his hand on Mark's shoulder playfully and continued, "If I didn't have Jodie already I'd be asking for some tips."

"And that is something I can't help you with, I'm sorry to say I don't know how I do it. This has happened in almost every bar I've ever worked in, I must send out some sort of aura to the ladies," he said laughing.

The night went on as quick as it began and the bar bustled with people drinking, eating and dancing. The music played on creating the perfect atmosphere for a great night out. As the night approached closing time and Patrick and the rest of the bar staff began clearing tables and the bar, the conversation flowed between him and Mark as though they had been friends for years. Patrick was glad that he was getting on so well with Mark.

"So, you work here full time, what else do you do?" asked Mark as they were stacking chairs and bar stools.

"Nothing, just this. We are kind of house plants me and Jodie, we like to chill out in the flat whenever we get the chance."

"You don't go out?" Mark sounded surprised.

"Not really. We go out for dinner and a few drinks every now and then, but like I said we like our home comforts." Patrick didn't want to talk about the church, he thought that it was best kept for another time.

"Well, whatever keeps you happy mate. I was thinking since I've just started we could go for a drink one night? Since we're going to be working together then might as well know who I'm working with. What do you say?" Mark had a huge grin on his face that made Patrick think he wasn't going to take no for an answer.

I've never been on a night out without Jodie before, Patrick thought to himself. *That sounds ridiculous.*

"Might do you both some good to do something separately," said Mark.

"Can I get back to you on that?"

"No bother mate, don't mean to put under pressure. Just thought it would be good for team building," he laughed.

Patrick collected his jacket and wallet from the staff room and turned out the lights. As he approached the door Mark was stood outside the main entrance to the bar smoking a small cigar. William had already left earlier in the night and asked Patrick to lock up. He punched the digits into the alarms keypad and went outside.

"How you getting home?" he asked Mark.

"Taxi mate. It's on its way. You?"

"Same. Just going to phone it now," Patrick took out his mobile phone from his jacket pocket. There were still people crowding the streets trying to order cabs and make their way home.

"I can drop you off if you want and we can split the fare?"

"Do you live far from Glasgow Harbour?" Patrick realised he didn't know.

"Not far," said Mark.

The taxi pulled up and Mark opened the door, cigar still in hand. The taxi driver called out from the front, "You can't smoke that in here mate!"

"Just putting it out now," he turned to Patrick. "You coming?"

"Yeah, why not? Thanks." Patrick climbed in and the taxi began its journey to Patrick and Jodie's flat.

Twelve

What if?

Jodie sat out in the small balcony. It was 2:15am and she couldn't sleep. Her head was filled with Patrick. She was worried about him, he seemed to be losing sleep over the situation he now found himself in and she was slightly anxious about his involvement now with the police. All sorts of scenarios were going through her head, causing her to lose sleep herself.

What if the killer knows that we are working alongside the police and is watching us? What if he knows where we live? What if Patrick gets hurt during all of this? What if there is another murder before the Police catch whoever it is? I'm scared about going out by myself now.

She hadn't mentioned any of this to Patrick, she didn't want him to be worrying about her when he had all of this going on in his head. She wished she could take it from him and she be the one that had to deal with it.

Even though it was summer, there was still a cold breeze flowing past. She sat on the wicker chair in the balcony and watched the night go by. She watched the odd car pass by and wondered if Patrick were on his way home yet. Just as she was about to go back inside the sound of a black taxi pulled up outside the main entrance to their building. Jodie leaned over the side to look down and saw Patrick get out of the taxi. She smiled and went inside to put the kettle on. The night was silent and she could hear Patrick climbing the set of stairs outside their front door. Then his key being turned in the lock.

"Hi," he called out quietly, aware of the neighbours. "What are you doing up at this time?" he asked putting his jacket on the coat hook next to the door.

"Couldn't sleep," Jodie replied. "How was your shift babe?" Jodie handed him a cup of tea and they both went into the living room.

"It was really good actually. A new guy started as a member of bar staff tonight. He was really nice." Patrick blew into the mug to cool the tea before taking a sip.

"What is his name?" Jodie fell backward on to the couch with fatigue.

"Mark something, can't remember his second name. He was behind the bar for a total of half an hour and some woman gave him a list of drinks and her phone number on the back, it was priceless," Patrick laughed as he recalled the moment.

Jodie seemed to be falling asleep on the couch but sat up to try to stay awake. "Sounds like a bit of a ladies man. Was he being cocky about it?"

"Not at all, just said he didn't know how he managed to do it. He asked if I wanted to go for a drink with him," Patrick said it like he was asking her permission.

"Well, what did you say? Did you say yes?" Jodie asked. She was a little unsure about Patrick going on a night out with someone he had only just met but she didn't want to sound like the type of person that told her man who they could and couldn't be friends with and why should she? Of course she trusted him, she trusted him with her life. They had been together long enough for her to know that they only had eyes for each other.

"Well I said to him to leave it with me and I'd let him know at a later date. I kind of wanted to know what you thought first," he admitted, "does that make me sound like a push over?"

Jodie thought about it for a moment. "Erm, yes a little," she smiled. "Although I would like to meet him first, make sure he is not a bad influence," she joked.

Patrick stood up and put his tea down on the floor next to the couch. He walked over to where Jodie was sitting and sat down enveloping her in his arms. She was cold to touch.

"Are you ok? You're freezing." Patrick hugged her tightly almost squeezing the breath out of her.

"Yeah, I'm fine I'm just worried about you. I mean, you're taking on this case with the police which I know for sure is stressing you out. I know you are not sleeping because you are worrying about letting them down and obviously your head is not your own," she almost forgot to breathe she said it so fast.

Patrick held her away from his body so he could see her face. "And obviously it's causing you some stress too. Jodie it's not as if I haven't experienced spirits before, just never ones this intense. Honestly, if it gets too much for me or for us I'll take it easy."

A few moments passed where they both said nothing. Then Jodie said, "I think you should go out with this Mark guy, it will be a good way for you to de-stress and have a bit if fun."

"I think so too," Patrick replied. "I will make arrangements the next time we are on shift together."

"Good," Jodie smiled gently.

Patrick kissed her softly on the nose, then on the lips. Patrick was able to put the worry to the back of Jodie's mind that night. As she fell asleep in his arms on the couch, he felt the presence of one of the girls enter the room. She put a fretful feeling into him and he couldn't shift it. He felt the weight of the world suddenly on his shoulders. He enjoyed his ability to communicate with spirits but at times he wished he could be as normal as anyone else and just get a good night sleep. The room turned icy cold and the hairs on Jodie's arms stood on end as she slept in Patrick's arms.

"I know you're anxious and I am going to help you but I am asking for some space tonight. I need to sleep," Patrick whispered into the empty space in the room.

The fretful feeling dispersed but the room stayed chilly for the remainder of the night into the early hours. Patrick decided to stay with Jodie and sleep in the living room, there was no point in waking her when she now seemed so peaceful.

As he drifted off, he thought of the investigation with the police.

Where are you, you son of a bitch? He thought to himself. *We'll find you and when we do you'll be sorry you were ever born.*

Patrick fell asleep with the feeling of anger and disgust in the pit of his stomach. He was going to find the man who murdered these girls, even if it killed him.

Thirteen

Be careful what you wish for

The darkness around him seemed to get darker the faster he ran and the faster he ran the further into nothing he seemed to get. Patrick felt like his lungs would burst and his legs would collapse with the speed.

He looked around and saw what seemed like a thousand miles of nothing. He ran towards the army of darkness and as he did he heard his footsteps repeating behind him. He tried to turn round to see who was behind him but when he did the footsteps fell behind him again! All he had was the urge to run faster until the footsteps, now louder, fell from his hearing. He heard a ringing sound, quiet at first, then it became louder and it rang persistently. He heard Jodie's voice, she was softly calling his name and he began to panic. *Run, run, run,* he tried to call out to her but she continued to say his name, over and over, a little more firmly now.

"Patrick? Patrick, its D.S Preston on the phone for you, get up!" she sounded annoyed now.

"What? Was I asleep?" he was confused and his heart pounded hard in his chest. He sat up on the couch and took the phone from Jodie, rubbing his eyes as he tried to adjust to his sudden conscious state.

"Hello?"

"Ah, Mr McLaughlin, it's D.S Preston here. I wanted to personally inform you that your D.N.A test proved negative. There were absolutely no traces of your D.N.A to evidence that you had any physical part in the murders of the three young women."

"I already knew that," Patrick said bluntly. He was feeling a little cranky from being awoken by the phone. "So, now what?"

"D.C Lang and I are making a few inquiries this afternoon regarding the Collins, Levine and Noble case, but before we do we'd like you to come down to the station. There are a few things we'd like to discuss with you beforehand."

"Ok, when?" Patrick's voice croaked.

"Can you be here for ten o'clock please?" It didn't sound like a question.

"Yeah that's not a problem. See you then."

Patrick hung up the phone and threw himself backwards onto the couch again. Jodie appeared over him holding a mug of hot coffee.

"You were restless during the night," she said. "Here," she handed him the mug as he sat up, "this will wake you up."

"I've to go into the Police station at ten to speak to Preston and Lang. My results came back negative." He stared into the mug as though he didn't know what it contained.

"What is wrong with you? You look like a zombie, and you were tossing and turning all night."

"Was I? I feel really tired and I had a really strange dream that I was being chased, but I couldn't see who I was running from," he shook his head. "I must be going mad," he smiled sarcastically.

"Well, whatever you are, you're going to be late if you don't get a move on," she tapped her watch and smiled guiltily. "Sorry, just don't want them thinking that you're not capable."

"I'm not so sure I am capable today. I feel like I've been banged over the head with a boulder," he squeezed his eyes shut and rubbed his head.

"Were you drinking last night after the shift finished? Could it be that?" Jodie suggested.

"No, there wasn't much time for a beer during clear up, plus I had the keys. I don't like being on lock up with a drink in me."

Patrick stood up, walked to the bathroom and switched on the shower. He climbed in and turned the power up to jet and the temperature up to high. He stood there for ten minutes to wake himself up.

Jodie sat down on the spot where Patrick had been just moments before. The worry she had the night before came flooding back. The dreams, the sleepless nights and the constant visions and voices were seriously wearing him down and Jodie was beginning to feel the strain and stress Patrick was feeling. He was putting on such a brave front for all that was going on.

The last thing he needs is me stressing him out with how I feel about it all. I just wish that I could at least take some of what he was experiencing for just a while, she thought to herself fretfully.

Jodie picked up the mug and started towards the kitchen when suddenly she felt like she was burning. Her skin began to tingle painfully and she broke out in a sweat. There came a pain in her chest that was like nothing she had ever experienced before in her life. She felt like her lungs were filling up and she couldn't get a proper breath. She tried to stay calm and move to the kitchen to get some water but she felt like she was being held back. Her right ankle began to throb as though her bones had been fractured by an unknown force.

Overwhelmed by the pain and burning sensation, Jodie collapsed. Patrick heard a thud from the living room as he passed after stepping out of the shower, to find Jodie lying on the floor.

"Oh my god Jodie what's wrong?" he ran to her side.

There was no response. Patrick dropped to his knees and held her in his arms, "Jodie, Jodie..."

She opened her eyes and looked up to see absolute terror in his face.

"Why are we on the floor?" she asked calmly, feeling her face against his chest, still wet from the shower.

"You fainted. What happened?" the panic in his voice faded a little once Jodie responded.

"Uh, I don't know," she sat up straight. "I went to go to the kitchen and I began to feel like my body was on fire. I literally felt like my skin was burning. I couldn't breathe Patrick. And my ankle felt like it was being crushed. It was horrible, it happened so suddenly."

"It sounds like you had an anxiety or panic attack and a bad one at that. You should see a doctor Jodie."

"No, honestly I feel better. I'll just rest now. You go and do what you have too to help the police with the case. Seriously I will be fine," she smiled reassuringly at him.

"Not a chance Jodie I'm taking you to the doctor now, there is no way I am leaving you after what just happened."

Patrick picked up the phone and called the station to inform them that he would be in later in the afternoon once he had taken Jodie to the doctor to be checked over.

"Mr McLaughlin we appreciate that your fiancée seems to be ill but we have a very serious case on our hands here and you are supposed to be assisting us in our enquiries," D.S Preston stressed.

"Yes I am assisting you D.S Preston but this is also very important to me sir and I will be with you no later than one o'clock. I promise you that."

"Ok, well I expect you will keep your word on this Mr McLaughlin," Preston eased off.

"I will, and D.S Preston?"

"Yes?"

"Please call me Patrick. You make me feel old when you refer to me as Mr McLaughlin."

Fourteen

Warnings

"See? I told you I was fine," said Jodie as they left the doctors surgery.

Patrick shook his head. "You are not fine Jodie. The Doctor said that you had an anxiety attack due to stress and lack of sleep. That does not say fine to me that says that there is something you are not telling me and I want to know what it is."

"What's that supposed to mean?" she stopped walking.

"What exactly are you so stressed about that you aren't sleeping?"

Jodie sighed and continued walking at a slower pace. She spoke quietly as they walked to the taxi rank near the surgery.

"I am stressed about you, all this police stuff and enquiries and *your* lack of sleep is worrying me Patrick. I am worried about *your* mental wellbeing. Don't you agree that this is a little stressful for both of us?"

Patrick felt bad for the way he insinuated that she was keeping something from him. "Of course I agree. But it's something that I have to do Jodie. For one, I can't just ignore messages, you know yourself that if you do that they don't leave you alone, even if they are just minor. And two, I'm getting a lot of information at one time and when I'm trying to rest my mind at night that's when I am more open and receptive to these spirits. I can't help it Jodie. You of all people should know that!"

Both seemed quiet for a while afterwards. They got into a taxi and it drove them back to their flat in Glasgow Harbour. Patrick helped Jodie upstairs to their door.

"I understand that you're helping the Police and that you would never ignore the messages that you get. But I am allowed to worry about you aren't I?" said Jodie.

"Of course you are babe. Come here," he wrapped his arms around her and gave her a tight hug. "I love you, you know that don't you?"

"I love you too, just look after yourself. I know it's awful what happened to those girls and I am proud to say that you are going to help track down their killer. But please remember that you have a life here to come back to. I don't want our abilities to come between us Patrick."

"They won't Jodie, I promise you that. I have to go, I'm meeting D.S Preston and D.C Lang in thirty minutes at the station and they'll kick off if I am not on time."

He kissed Jodie on the head then ran down the stairs to get back into the taxi that had dropped them both off from the doctor surgery just a few minutes previously.

Jodie let herself into their flat. It was a hot day outside and the apartment was stuffy so she opened the sliding glass door and went out onto the balcony for air. There wasn't much of a breeze out there but Jodie felt like she was able to breathe and relax.

Scottish summers weren't much to write home about but if you were lucky the sun shone a few days between the months of May and September. Today was one of those days.

"Well Mr Sun, I may as well make the most of you whilst you have made the effort to visit us today," she said as she smiled up at the sky and went to the bedroom to get the book that she was reading.

She went back out to the living room and to her surprise the door to the balcony was closed. "I could have sworn I left that open," she said as she walked over to the door and opened it again. It made a loud scraping sound as it slid open.

"I would have definitely heard that closing!" she said aloud.

Jodie tried to ignore it and walked out onto the balcony again. She sat down on the sun lounger that Patrick had bought in case the sun happened to shine like this day and opened her book.

In front of their building was the expressway leading in and out of Glasgow city centre and Jodie could hear all of the traffic making its way up and down the road. The volume of traffic wasn't that high but enough that there was a loud hum as each vehicle passed. She could also hear the birds singing in the trees around her. They sounded happy, as if they were enjoying the sunshine, as was she. The clouds in the sky came few and far between. But when they were there, they were small and fluffy. The light from the sun bounced off them and they seemed to be whiter than white.

As Jodie observed all of these things around her she relaxed more and began to forget the anxiety attack and the worry she felt for Patrick. She began to drift off in her relaxed state. The birds still sang as she began to dream.

In her dream she walked along an empty street. All of the buildings were closed up for the night with the display windows sent little light into the street. She found it strange that birds should chirp happily when it was the middle of the night, but she was happy to listen all the same. It was mild in temperature and she was wearing a low cut black dress (which lay just above her knee) and black heels. She knew Patrick would love this outfit. But where was he?

She suddenly realised that she was alone. She began to feel nervous and knew that something wasn't right. She looked around her for any signs of life but there were only shadows in the alleyways and this made her feel very uncomfortable. She began to walk quicker but her legs would not carry her. She suddenly began to feel very tired and her head began to pound.

What's wrong with me? she thought to herself.

This is what he does Jodie, it's his way of slowing you down. Making you feel helpless and weak, a voice came from behind her.

Jodie spun round to see where the voice was coming from and what she saw sent shivers down her spine.

81

Oh my God, are you....?

Jodie knew that stood in front of her were the spirits of Rebecca Collins, Michelle Levine and Angela Noble. This was the first time in her life as a spiritualist medium she had ever come face to face with the spirit of someone before. She didn't know what to make of it.

This is what happened to us Jodie. He is one sick man, you have to trust us when we say you are not safe.

They all seemed to be speaking in sync with each other. Jodie tried to walk towards them but her legs felt like they were anchored to the ground.

What do you mean I'm not safe? Why am I not safe? Jodie seemed to be shouting, all the while her lips not moving.

You're not safe, nobody's safe. Their voices seemed distant, like their energies were fading.

Wait, I need more than that, you can't just say something like that then leave, she called out. She realised that even though she could hear them and they could hear her, no-one moved their lips, the voices, including her own were in her mind.

Suddenly she felt cold, and the girls were gone. She stood alone in the dark empty street where she had found herself communicating with the girls.

Now what? She asked herself. She looked down and felt a spine tingling sensation as the thought entered her mind. *We are all wearing the same type of clothes.*

They all wore similar black dresses, some may say revealing and some may say elegant, black high heels and gold jewellery.

Her thoughts were interrupted by ear piercing screams coming from three different directions from where she was stood. She watched as she saw the murders being replayed to her and she felt sick as she watched Rebecca, Michelle and Angela being strangled.

Who is it? Who is he? I can't see his face! She shouted out feeling helpless. She couldn't move. She felt her bones trembling inside her body and she cried as she watched in fear as the black silhouette murdered these three innocent beautiful women.

Rebecca stood next to her as Jodie looked on. She turned to Rebecca and said, *I couldn't see his face! I'm sorry, but I couldn't see his face!*

A tear dropped down Rebecca's face as she looked into Jodie's eyes.

You won't see his face till it's too late Jodie!

Jodie's own screams woke her up.

Fifteen

Inquiries

Caroline Stevens stood at the large bay window of the flat that she had once shared with Rebecca, she was quiet as she stared out to the busy traffic and people rushing up and down the street. A single tear dropped down her cheek as she wondered helplessly what had happened to her friend. The flat seemed so empty without her. Her bedroom lay exactly as it did on the night that she was killed. Caroline didn't want to touch anything, move anything or even go in. She felt like she wanted to leave it exactly the way it was the last time Rebecca was in it, that way it would feel like Rebecca was still around. There were a few photo frames around the living room with pictures of Rebecca and Caroline in them. The television played silently in the corner with no viewer and there were newspaper cuttings of the murder cases piled on the coffee table. Caroline Stevens was a mess and had become obsessed with her friends murder.

The buzzer rang in the hallway and Caroline picked it up.

"Hello?" Caroline had stopped buzzing people into the building without checking who it was first since Rebecca had been murdered.

"Caroline Stevens? This is D.S Preston from Strathclyde Police, we spoke on the phone?"

"Yes, please do come up."

Even though she knew who was climbing the stairs she couldn't help shiver when she heard the echoing footsteps ascending the close outside the front door. She opened the door on the chain to check for sure.

"Could I see some I.D please?" Caroline said quietly.

Preston and Lang both showed their badges clearly and Caroline let the chain off the door and welcomed them in. She led them into the living room and offered tea.

"That would be lovely Miss Stevens, milk and two for me," Lang smiled.

As she made tea in the kitchen, Preston, Lang and Patrick all sat in the living room of what was once Rebecca Collins' home.

"Getting anything Patrick?" Lang asked sarcastically.

Patrick looked at him and rolled his eyes. He looked around the living space that Caroline once shared with Rebecca and felt a great sadness for those who had been killed and those who had been left behind.

"Well if I was picking up anything you'd be the last person I'd tell for your sarcastic manner, *Sir*." Patrick walked over to the couch and sat down whilst they all waited for Caroline to come back from the kitchen.

Preston elbowed Lang in the ribs, not so hard that it hurt but hard enough to let him know that he didn't appreciate his tone towards Patrick.

"Just remember why we are all working together on this case Lang. Be professional please, the pair of you."

Caroline entered the room carrying a tray with tea cups and a plate of chocolate biscuits.

"Sorry, I don't have any doughnuts in the house," she gave a slight smile.

Patrick heard a laugh that sounded like it was coming from another room, but it was in his head. He kept it to himself.

"Before we start, can I ask your medium here a question?" she asked.

"By all means," Lang tucked into a chocolate biscuit, secretly hoping that she was going to be as sceptical towards Patrick as he was.

Caroline sat opposite Patrick and stared deep into his eyes. Patrick felt like she was looking for something inside his head. Maybe she was.

"Do you really believe that you can help this case? I mean, if psychic mediums could do what you all say, then why haven't you just come up with a name yet? Why do you have to investigate with the police? If you really were psychic then wouldn't it be like... picking a name out of the air?" Caroline sounded irritated.

Lang had to suppress a smile raising the corners of his mouth. Another nudge came from Preston's elbow, harder this time.

"Well, if Rebecca knew the name of her killer then I'm sure that she would be able to tell me..." Patrick answered sincerely.

Caroline blurted out, "But she did, he introduced himself at the pub that night!"

"Miss Stevens, who are you referring too?" Preston gently interrupted.

"The guy who I tried to get her to talk to, he was sat at the end of the bar we were in and he kept staring at her. I told her to give him a chance, but then I left," she began to cry.

"Let's start from the beginning shall we?" Lang brought out his note pad and pen and sat patiently waiting for Caroline to compose herself to tell her version of the events leading up to Rebecca's murder.

"So, the male you met in the bar, what bar was this?" Lang began.

"My House," Caroline said quietly.

"Ok, and was it busy?" Preston added.

"Erm, not really, I'd say there were around fifty odd people there, but it was early." Caroline's expression showed that she was searching her brain for accurate answers.

"Do you have reason to believe that the man would want to harm Rebecca?" Preston added.

"Well, it's a little coincidental that Rebecca meets a guy on the same night she ends up strangled to death."

"That may well be true Caroline but at this point we cannot rule out the possibility that someone else could be involved," Preston jotted some notes down in his book also.

Caroline went on to describe Ross Turner, the man who remained nameless to all of them at this point. Preston and Lang took down a description of him, clothing, height, hair colour etc.

Patrick made his own notes for some experiments that he planned to carry out later on that evening.

"We will investigate any CCTV footage from the bar on the night in question Miss Stevens and we will be in touch," Preston said as they were shown to the door.

Caroline looked at Patrick who was standing at the top of the landing and could see that he was somewhere else. Patrick could see Rebecca standing behind Caroline in the frame of the door. She seemed faint, almost like he could see right through her. She had a worried expression on her face. Patrick tried to put it to the back of his head for the time being.

"We will do our best to catch this person Caroline," he said.

Please do, before someone else gets hurt. It was Rebecca who replied to Patrick's words.

Sixteen

The invisible man

Patrick, Preston and Lang walked down the stairs in silence after questioning Caroline Stevens. It wasn't till they got into the car that Preston turned to face Patrick and said, "So what kind of stuff were you picking up in there? And don't tell me nothing I could see it in your face that you were getting something."

Patrick saw Lang roll his eyes in the rear view mirror and he tuned to face him too.

"For god sake, I feel like I'm the criminal here," he laughed it off.

"Well?" Preston pushed.

"Yes, I did pick up a few things in the flat and I took some notes of my own, so that I don't forget any details."

"So do we have to use the torture technique or are you going to tell us willingly?" Lang said.

You're a pain in my neck Lang, Patrick thought to himself before he replied. "I saw Rebecca, not very clearly, but she did speak to me." He waited for a sarcastic response from Lang. When it didn't come he continued. "She said that she wants us to solve this so that nobody else gets hurt."

"Ok, so what is your next step?" Preston seemed genuinely interested. Lang listened purely out of curiosity as to what Patricks reply would be.

"Forgive me if I am wrong but shouldn't *I* be asking that question, you are the police after all?" Patrick said.

"And forgive me if I'm wrong," Lang started, "but aren't you the psychic who said you could help solve this?"

Preston sighed loudly through frustration and said, "Are we really going to do this?"

Lang turned back to face the windscreen and said nothing.

"I am going to conduct a few experiments," Patrick felt numb. Nervousness took over him, a feeling of scrutiny from both officers. He knew Lang was probably a lost cause, but he was surprised by Preston's persistence however, he knew that Preston was much more on side than Lang was and probably ever would be.

He hadn't felt like this since before he met Jodie all those years ago. For the first time in years he was going to have to prove himself to a complete sceptic and he knew it was going to be a hell of a job.

The fact that he had to do it through helping to solve a murder case was making him feel physically sick.

What if I fail? What if I cannot find them the justice they deserve? he thought.

"What kind of experiments?" Lang asked, not turning to face him as he spoke.

"Well I was thinking of trying automatic writing, and perhaps if that isn't enough then a séance?" *That sounded like I was asking permission,* he thought to himself.

"Do we have to be there?" Lang sounded a little concerned now.

"Of course we do, we need to see the proof that he is genuine so we can report back to the DCI in charge," Preston said.

"You're not scared are you?" Patrick mocked and Preston laughed.

"Don't be stupid, of course I'm not, I just think it's a whole lot of shit that I can't be bothered with!" Lang turned to face Patrick again, almost as if he was defending himself against the mocking and Preston laughed as he switched on the engine.

"Look, I can tell that you are not entirely happy about my involvement Jim, but I have my own spiritualist church. You are both welcome to come tonight and sit through a service. No need to participate, just to watch and see what this is all about," he said flicking through his notes.

"We will be there Patrick, just name the place." Preston put the car into first and pulled out of their parking space.

As they drove back to the station Patrick began to think about Jodie. He thought about how this was affecting her and he worried that it might be too much on their relationship.

But she understands this more than anyone. Surely she will be able to cope with all the stress that this could lead to. He thought to himself.

As they pulled into the station Preston turned to Patrick and said, "So I think you probably have all that you need from today, why don't you go home and prepare what you need to for tonight and we will meet you at the spiritualist church. Please do not mention to anyone that you are helping out with a murder investigation. We don't want the press following you around for information."

"No problem, here is the address. Be there for around eight o'clock, I'll sign you both in." Patrick handed him a piece of paper with the address on it and he got out of the car.

"What do you mean you will *sign* us in?" asked Lang just before Patrick closed the car door.

"Well, you need to be a member of the church to get in but as I am the president of the church then I will be able to sign you in." Patrick closed the door and tapped the top of the car as Preston pulled away to park in the car park.

"I didn't know he was the president of a spiritualist church." Lang sounded a little freaked out by this point.

"I told you to give him a chance. He wouldn't be the president if he didn't know what he was doing." Preston laughed at Lang's expression. "It will be fine, trust him to get the information we need to find this guy. I know he won't let us down."

"You have a lot of faith, I'll give you that."

"In situations like this you have to. We don't have much of a lead on this case and if Patrick can get us what we need then he will get all my praise!"

"What if he doesn't?" asked Lang doubtfully as Preston parked the car and got out.

Preston regarded this for a moment and took out a pack of cigarettes from his inside pocket. He lit one and dragged on it for a few seconds. He threw his head back and blew the smoke up toward the now cloudy sky. "Then we hope to Jesus that the DNA samples bring us something."

For the first time during this case Preston felt genuine concern that this case was going to be one of the hardest to solve.

"We also still have to check the CCTV from 'My House,' where Rebecca met that guy, according to Caroline." Lang tried to reassure. He could see the stress in Preston's face.

"Hmm. Fingers crossed it reveals a face, then the press can release the images, see if we can rake up any more witnesses."

He took another long drag on the cigarette and held it in his lungs. It seemed to slow things down, give him time to think.

"At the moment this murderer seems untraceable," said Lang.

Preston stamped on the end of the cigarette and crushed it into the ground. He looked at Lang and said, "And if it continues that way, this case will fold."

Seventeen

An unexpected visitor

As Ross flipped the bacon, the piping hot fat from the frying pan spattered onto his skin and he felt his stomach nip a little. The kitchen smelled like a burger van, the kind you would find outside a football stadium or at a theme park. He was making a fry up for himself and the television played in the background. The sun shone through the window and it showed every speck of dirt on the glass. The floor around the cooker had spatters of cooking fat on it and the worktops were also quite greasy looking. He finished cooking the bacon, sausage and eggs and served them on a heavily buttered role. He walked into the living room and sat down on the chair facing the television.

He was not really watching the programme, he was just staring at the screen, thinking of his next plan.

He smiled as he thought of his next victim, thinking of how he could add to his technique to throw the police off track.

That's if they're even on track. He thought to himself.

As he ate he pictured Rebecca, Angela and Michelle. He was not ashamed of what he had done. Why should he be? He was only doing it for the good of his sanity.

"Billy fucked us up. It's only necessary that I put things right, isn't it?" he said as he looked at the picture of his mum on the kitchen wall.

Ross Turner had started out his life as best he could, considering his mother was a beaten wife and his father was a drunken waste of a human being, in Ross's opinion.

After Billy had gone to jail, Ross slowly became insane, but he knew that the grief for his mother had taken over. The revenge had become an obsession. It was the first thing that he thought about on awakening and the last thing before slipping into sleep at night.

His life had become about living for his mother. Prison wasn't justice enough for Ross after the murder, torture and mental abuse that Maria had endured for many years of her marriage to Billy. That's what he wanted, justice. He knew deep down that all of the pain, loss and frustration he felt for his mother was one hundred percent down to Billy, but he just couldn't accept the fact that Maria was gone, and Billy was in prison, still alive. He had convinced himself that someone else was to blame. All of those horrible women who smelled of cigarette smoke and alcohol that Billy brought home, all of the lies, all of the dirty filthy lies that seemed to pour out of his mouth with great ease, it all became unbearable for Ross.

Angela Noble became part of Ross's revenge, the first *real* piece of sanity brought back to his grief stricken mind.

Angela Noble looked like all that he could remember of Billy's conquests. Typical looking girl out to hurt and cause carnage on someone else. But he knew that if a Billy came along, she wouldn't hesitate to make it known that she was up for it.

It all seemed like it was meant to be, the sun was setting and the beer garden was beginning to empty as the night began to cool down and a slight chill in the Glasgow night air sent goose bumps over the skin of the people enjoying their martini's and vodka's. For some reason Angela was sat outside on her own, with a black maxi dress and long brunette hair that had natural curls hanging around her face and down her back.

One may have said she was elegantly presented, but not Ross. For some reason, when he looked at her, he felt sheer rage. It all happened in a blur, Ross felt like he wasn't the one committing the crime, but a witness to it. A witness who enjoyed watching her squirm in a chokehold, a hold that she hoped she would be able to escape and a hold that he knew he would never let go. Not until he was satisfied that the job was done, keeping in mind, a job that he hadn't even *planned* to do, on that occasion anyway.

It wasn't until he saw the local news the next evening that the real satisfaction kicked in. The satisfaction of knowing that, in his mind, causing grief was to cure grief, his own grief. The grief he felt for Maria. But the pain was still there, he could feel her pain, he could feel how she felt when she heard Billy bring home the latest whore.

One is not enough justice for my mother, he kept telling himself.

He felt no remorse for Angela and neither for Michelle or Rebecca.

"There will never be enough justice for you mum. They'll suffer the way we did, until I take my last breath, until I bleed my last drop, whatever it takes."

The buzzer rang in Ross' hallway and for a moment he wondered if this was the end of his run already. Well, if it was, he wasn't ready, but he wasn't going to show it on the surface. He walked steadily from the kitchen to the hall and picked up the receiver, picking up some post that had been dropped on to the mat at the same time.

"Hello?"

"Son?" A familiar but gruff voice replied.

Ross was in disbelief. *There's no way.*

"Ross?" Billy's voice was clearer now than it ever had been. He felt like a child again. The fear of not knowing what to expect had crept over his skin like a colony of ants.

Do not let him hear your fear, he can't win you over with his intimidation, you owe it to yourself.

"I'm sorry, but may I ask, what the *fuck* you think you are doing here?" Ross hissed into the receiver.

"I just want to talk to you son, please I need to explain a few things, please let me in?" Billy sounded remorseful.

"I'm not your son, and no, you can't come in. Are you fucking stupid?"

Billy stood outside the secure door flat and took a deep breath. He didn't expect anything else from Ross and why should he? He had been the cause of his mother's death, although not physically, mentally, yes. He had admitted a very long time ago that the lies, cheating and abuse had sent her over the edge and she had killed herself, which he had been riddled with guilt from ever since.

Billy had been seeing a councillor for his state of mind and his time in prison had made him believe he was now a changed man. All Billy wanted was to at least explain what had made him the man he was back then and if Ross would let him he would try to amend his mistakes.

Billy knew fine well that Ross wasn't going to speak to him, never mind let him in his home, but he didn't want the what if, question running through his mind until his dying day. He rang the buzzer again. No answer.

He pushed the door, on the off chance that it would open. It didn't. He turned his back to the door to face Dumbarton Road in Partick. The street was still busy for eight o'clock at night. The sun was still shining and the roads still hummed with cars and double deck buses. He looked out at the street in front of him and Billy knew that he had to walk away. There were no second chances for men like him, changed or not.

He turned to face the door at the sound of it opening and much to his disbelief, standing in the doorway was Ross.

Eighteen

A convenient accident

"You've got ten minutes," Ross said.

"OK."

As they climbed the stairs of the close, Ross wondered what on earth Billy was going to say that he thought would make things better.

Nothing could make things better between us, he thought to himself.

The close was lit with dim bulbs which looked as though they were from the war years, and the stench of bleach was overwhelming. As they climbed higher, the smell became stronger, and there came a clanging sound from above them.

"What's with the smell and the noise?" Billy hoped to break the silence as they climbed the stairs.

"One of the neighbours is mopping the floors of the close," Ross answered bluntly.

"It's nice that someone looks after the close isn't it?"

Ross blocked out Billy's voice and opened his front door. He wanted to jam Billy's head between the door and the door frame as he entered but thought better of it.

He followed Ross into the living room and stood by the window. Ross looked at him expectantly, but Billy said nothing. He looked around and saw the picture of Maria, his late wife and felt a wave of guilt flow through him. When he looked up and saw Ross staring into his eyes, he felt frozen, like he had forgotten everything he had planned to say.

"Well, aren't you going to tell me how sorry you are? How sorry you are about Mum, about how you treated us?" Ross taunted him.

"Would it make a difference? You wouldn't listen to me anyway."

"You owe me some sort of fucking explanation. My Mum killed herself and left me and you drove her to it." Ross spoke through gritted teeth. "Oh, and while we are on the subject of driving her to do things that were not necessary, you should know that she made sure I found out about him."

Billy's face changed from self pity and regret to confusion. "Him, who?"

"Jeffery? You remember him don't you *Dad*? Your *first* born son?" Ross continued taunting him.

"How do you know about that?" Billy asked quietly.

"Mum left me a note. And she made sure that I would find it. I know all about how you made her give him up for adoption. How she felt like she had no other choice but to get rid of him."

"I..." Billy did not have anything to say regarding Jeffery. He knew that it was there and then that Ross did not regard him as anything else but a monster.

"You what?"

"Nothing, all I was going to say was what I have already said. But there would be no point, my words will not provide any comfort."

"Do you know what? I don't even know this Jeffery person and I am already jealous of him. In fact, I actually quite dislike him." Ross took a step closer to Billy, now standing so close that Billy could feel his son's breath on his face.

"Why is that?" Billy asked.

"Because the lucky bastard is free from you, he didn't have to live his life watching you beat his Mother like she was some kind of wild animal. He didn't have to grow up with *you* as a Dad. He got the get out of jail free card... and I got a fucking life sentence!"

A few moments passed where silence was the only thing that filled the room.

"I wasn't a well man Ross. I was an alcoholic and off my face on coke most of the time. It wasn't...."

97

"Wasn't, what? Wasn't your fault? You're so full of it. I don't give a shit what you were on, she was my Mum, your wife. What man treats his wife and family the way you did? You beat her black and blue for years and shagged anything you could get your filthy hands on, and you subjected us *both* to it!" Ross's rage had gone past boiling point and he slammed Billy up against the wall.

All sorts of thoughts raced through his mind, his Mum, his childhood. He felt like he couldn't breathe, his throat felt like it was closing up slowly and his vision became blurred.

"Go on then, if it makes you feel better!" Billy shouted in his face. "Punch me, slam my head off the wall. Do what you will but it will never change what I did, it will never bring her back!"

Ross let go of Billy and turned his back on him. He tried to calm himself, he didn't want his neighbours hearing anything. He couldn't risk it. He took a few deep breathes as Billy looked on, wondering what was coming next.

"All I wanted was to tell you how sorry I am and if I could take it all back I would."

"But you can't, so what's the point of coming here and causing me more misery?" he turned to Billy, his face expressionless.

"I didn't want to go through the rest of my life wondering, what if?"

They stood in silence for a few moments more, both thinking about what life would have been like if Billy hadn't done what he did for all those years.

"I think you should leave before I do something that I will regret!" Ross looked straight through Billy, knowing that if pushed far enough, he would break his neck and that would be it done!

"OK, I'll leave, but I am truly sorry."

He walked to the front door and as he left he didn't look back. Billy knew his bridges were well and truly burnt.

I've ruined him, he thought to himself as he descended the stairs of the close.

He passed the woman who was mopping the floor and the smell of bleach was once again overwhelming. She smiled at him as he passed her on the stairs and he smiled back. She was an older lady, in her seventies with short white hair and an apron over her clothes.

"Watch your step there sir, it's awfully slippery," she warned him with a gentle voice.

"Thanks," Billy replied.

She watched him go down the next flight until he was no longer in her sight. She carried on mopping the cold granite flooring until she was interrupted by an echoing racket coming from below her and a male scream. The bumping and banging continued for a few more seconds as she made her way down. She guessed what had happened but what she found was not what she had expected.

She stood above him, half way down the set of stairs where he had met his maker. A broken neck, ankle twisted and facing the completely wrong way and an expression of terror as he lay there dead, eyes open facing the woman who had inevitably caused his death.

She began to scream uncontrollably until she found a young man stood next to her, Ross.

"Oh dear, call an ambulance," the woman held onto Ross as she spoke.

"Look's like he is dead," Ross replied.

"Oh my God, it's my fault. Please call an ambulance!"

Ross ran up to his flat to use the phone. He was in disbelief and also he felt like he was dreaming. He had wished his Father dead all this time and it had finally happened without him having to lay a finger on him.

That's karma for you, he thought to himself.

He dialled...

"Ambulance please, a man has fallen down the stairs in my building. I think he is dead," he smiled as he spoke.

Nineteen

A medium's proof

The church hall was beginning to fill up fast. Patrick and Jodie had laid out the seats for their guests and made sure that the room was set up for the evening demonstrations.

Preston and Lang had arrived a little before eight o'clock so as to blend in with the crowd and they came dressed as normal people would, not police officers.

"I cannot believe that I am even attempting this," Lang sniggered.

"Why?" Preston asked.

"Well, I'm one hundred percent not into all this nonsense and I think it's a waste of time."

"Well in that case why don't you ask the boss if he could transfer you on to another case because lets face it, right now this is all we have," Preston sounded aggravated.

"I'm not saying I want out of this case, I just don't trust Patrick."

"Yeah, you've made that pretty clear. Just go with it eh? I wouldn't have put my neck on the line with the boss if I didn't think that Patrick was capable of helping us in this alright?"

Both officers stayed quiet whilst more hopeful people poured through the doors of West End Spiritualist Church. Lang looked at the individual faces of those who had turned up at the church, hoping to get a message from a loved one from the other side. People took their seats as Patrick and Jodie took their places on the stage of the hall.

The hall was very large with high ceilings and a large chandelier in the middle. One bulb was out and there were nine others dimly lit.

Suppose that's to set the eerie mood then? Lang sniggered to himself. He looked around as he and Preston took their seats in the audience and saw that everyone had become silent and were now facing the stage.

"Good evening everyone. As some of you may or may not know my name is Patrick McLaughlin and this is my fellow medium, Jodie Jenkins. Tonight we will be trying our very best to get the messages to you that you wish to hear."

Lang sat back in his seat and listened.

"If Jodie or I come to you with a message, please answer in a clear voice yes or no. The spirits will link with your voice so we need you to be loud and as clear as you can."

Patrick looked at Jodie.

"If you have not been to anything like this before could you raise your hand?" Jodie spoke.

Lang suddenly saw Preston's hand raise along with a few others and realised that he himself had never been to anything like this before. He unwillingly raised his hand.

"OK, can I ask you Sir," she pointed to Lang. "What you hope to take away with you from this evening?"

Lang felt a little intimidated, like he was the only sceptical character in the hall. He looked at Preston who was suppressing a smile. Now he felt incredibly irritated.

"Hmm, I'd like some proof of the living dead I suppose," he said trying to disguise the irritable tone.

"You're not a believer in spirits Sir?" Jodie asked.

"I've yet to be convinced."

Jodie smiled at him and said, "OK sir, let's see if we can then."

Jodie continued talking to the crowd as Preston failed to hide his grin. He turned to Lang and said, "I think she did that on purpose."

"You're damn right she did. She's obviously been talking to Patrick about my scepticism and decided to take the piss right out of me."

"Oh shut up. Just listen to them and let's hope that we get something to work with from it." Preston turned to face the stage again.

The room was silent and Jodie stood utterly still as she and Patrick opened their minds to let the spirits channel their energies. Patrick looked straight ahead, without making eye contact with any member of the audience. He began to speak.

"Alright, I'm picking up on a baby in spirit," Patrick said.

The silence already within the room felt like it had turned to a still picture as everyone listened intently.

"I'm seeing an older man in spirit, claiming to have the spirit of a baby who passed only three days after touching the earth plane. Can anyone take the name George?" Patrick asked.

Then suddenly he shot a look at Lang, whose face had gone a whiter shade of pale.

Lang cleared his throat before he spoke. "I think I can."

"I have George here Sir. I want to place him as your father?" Patrick continued.

"Yes that's correct," he said loudly.

Preston was in disbelief now, he stared back and forth at Patrick and Lang as they both spoke.

"I'm forced to believe that the baby your father is claiming to have is your son, Sir?"

Lang contemplated this for a few seconds. *This is bloody ridiculous, why am I even answering these stupid questions?* he thought to himself.

"Can you take that Sir?" Patrick pressed.

"I don't know, maybe." Lang sounded uncertain but in the pit of his stomach he knew exactly what was coming next.

"Sir, I'm being shown two hospital rooms here," Patrick paused for a few seconds and paced the stage as he took the message, "I am seeing a car accident, your wife and father?"

Lang suddenly felt sick. Patrick was touching a nerve that hadn't been touched for a long time. He thought back to that fateful day when his Father's car collided with a truck on the M8 motorway, the car that carried his Wife, unborn child and his Father.

"Yes, there was a car accident involving them," he said. He thought to himself, *but* you're *telling* me *this, I am not telling you. You're getting the minimum out of me.*

"I also have the name James, can you take that?" Patrick asked.

"Yes."

"Your baby son James is with your father George. He has given you this message. He wants you to know that they are both ok and that he is very sorry for what happened."

Lang thought about this for a few moments. His heart pounded so hard he could feel it in his throat. "Any chance you could go into more detail?"

"Are you sure you want me to open it up in a public meeting?" Patrick asked him.

"Well if you can, then why not?" Lang tried to keep his scepticism at the surface. He didn't want Patrick thinking he had broken him down already.

"OK, if you wish. I'm being told that fifteen years ago, your Father and your Wife were going to visit some family. You couldn't be there as you had to work. It was a very sunny morning and the sun glare was overwhelming. Your father was driving and the sun had interfered with his ability to see the road ahead. He swerved slightly, but enough to collide with the truck coming up the right side of him. Your father slammed on the breaks and a car went into the back end of his. This caused your wife's waters to break and your father was left unconscious from his head being hit off the side window then the steering wheel. They were rushed to hospital where your Father died shortly afterwards and your wife gave birth to a baby boy, James, after you. Three days later your baby died in hospital, related to the car accident," Patrick stopped. He knew that he had said enough.

Preston looked at Lang. One tear dropped from his left eye and he wiped it away with his sleeve.

"Jim, you ok?" Preston put a hand on his shoulder.

"I need air," Lang got up and walked out of the hall.

Patrick nodded at Preston to go after him. He watched as Preston left the hall and motioned at Jodie to take over the demonstrations.

"OK ladies and gentlemen I'm going to take over whilst Patrick has a break."

Patrick followed Preston outside to the front of the church. He watched as Lang lit a cigarette and held the smoke in his lungs for what seemed like forever.

"Are you ok?" Patrick asked.

"How the *hell* did you know all that?" Lang asked angrily "Did you do some kind of research on my family or something? I mean, seriously what the hell..."

"You know how I do it. You just don't want to believe it."

"Patrick I think we'll call it a night, I think we got what we came for," Preston said.

"Did you get what you came for?" Patrick asked Lang.

Lang considered this for a moment. Had he got what he came for? To be reminded of his son and father's tragic deaths? The message had frightened him to say the least, but if anything else it convinced him that there was something else out there.

"Well, I think I got more than I needed. I'll hold my hands up Patrick, you've left me feeling rather amazed," he held his hand out to Patrick. "Looks like you're a legit part of our team now Mr McLaughlin."

"So you're converted then Jim?" Preston asked.

"Well wouldn't you be after experiencing that? Oh and by the way, I still want to see this automatic writing you were going on about! That would be interesting to see."

"Why not now?" Patrick asked.

Lang looked at Preston then back to Patrick. "Not tonight, I've seen enough. But definitely tomorrow at some point."

Preston smiled and felt a sense of relief as Lang and Patrick shook hands.

Twenty

Dreams of fire

Back in their home at Glasgow Harbour, Patrick and Jodie had settled down for the night and were on the couch watching the television. Jodie stared at the screen and could hear Patrick gently laughing, but as she watched her brain did not absorb the information coming from the characters in front of her. Instead her thoughts were overloaded with what seemed like fog and the thickness clouded her consciousness.

She had zoned out from reality and not realised it. She was in a small room, it was dull outside. She looked out of the window and could see that the sky had clouded over. The clouds were thick and looked heavy, like they were dropping down from the sky. The room was cool and the walls were grey, but not due to the decor. She tried to see what was on the walls of the small room but she couldn't, her vision seemed to be blurred.

Why?

There was a small desk across from her in the far corner and there was a computer lamp on it. She stood up and walked slowly over to the desk and switched on the lamp to see if this would help her to see. As she switched on the lamp she understood why her vision was blurry, the room was filled with smoke.

But I can't smell it, she thought to herself. She turned to see the rest of the room and walked to the window. As she looked out she couldn't see anything, just a blackness of nothing. She felt a wave of panic wash over her whole body. All of a sudden she felt hot and the heat crept from her toes all the way up her body. Not just the kind of hot you might feel on a sticky summers day as you make your way through crowds of people when shopping in town or in rush hour first thing in the morning on your way to work. No, this was different, like *oven hot!* It was as though she had opened one of those industrial ovens in kitchens that cater for hundreds of people every night in hotels and restaurants and the heat instantly fills the room and you immediately start to sweat.

"I have to get out of here, I don't feel well at all," she said aloud, it helped to keep her calm, speaking to the empty room.

As she looked around for a door, she found that it was boarded up, with ten inch nails and thick solid wood.

"What the hell is going on?" she screamed out. Just as she did, she noticed what was covering the walls in the dull grey colour. She inched closer and looked on at what was now the answer to her question. Jodie was reading intricate details about Angela Noble, Michelle Levine and Rebecca Collins deaths, from newspaper cuttings and hand written notes! As she scanned over them, she came across a picture of herself, a photo with her name on it!

"Oh my god," she backed away from the wall covered in photos and writing. "How the hell did they get a picture of me?"

She turned around and as she did she screamed out, "Is that it, am I next you sick freak? Well come on then... I'm here now! Get it done if you really want to!"

She was in the killer's bedroom and there was no way out! She began to feel sick at the thought of what was happening. The room began to spin and she found a bin just in time before she began to vomit. As she wretched the blood came in thick clumps and she felt weak not only at the sight of her own blood but at the realisation that she was not breathing.

Then the fire came, it crept in through every crack in the wall, ceiling and floor. It came in through the holes punched in the wood boarding the door by the ten inch nails and under the door frame.

Her skin began feeling like it was being cooked. She tried to scream for help, but nothing came from her throat. She tried to crawl to the window in the hope that it would open, but then remembered there was nothing out there, only blackness.

She felt a hand on the back of her neck as she tried to crawl, and assumed the worst. She tried to speak but her lungs were filled with smoke. She began to shake, violently and fast. She looked up and was relieved to see Patrick's face, his face filled with terror, shouting at her.

"Jodie, wake up, wake up!"

She opened her eyes. She gasped for air and held onto Patrick for dear life. She sucked in the air deep and long and tried to see him through tear filled eyes.

I'm awake, she thought. *I'm alive.*

Twenty One

Karma

Karma, the consequence of one's actions. Good deeds or wrong doings, selfish acts of greed or selfless acts of kindness. It's that old idea that he who reaps the benefits in selfish acts or inflicts harm and cruelty for any kind of reason to benefit himself will experience that, 'what goes around comes around,' feeling, at some point in their lives.

Of course it speaks the same words for those who do well in the world. Those who are helpful, kind to strangers, raise money for charity etc...

Those are the people who will experience kind 'rewards' if you like. Those are the people who will lead good, healthy and happy lives.

Whatever way you look at it, karma had taken its place in Ross' flat today. Billy was dead and Ross didn't even have to touch him to make it happen.

"A freak accident," the paramedic had quietly said to his colleague as they carried Billy out in the stretcher.

Yes, an accident waiting to happen, Ross had thought to himself and a very convenient one at that. All Ross had ever wanted was justice for Maria and her premature death. Justice was something Ross had dreamed about for years. But karma was beginning to sound so much better. Justice was everyone's human right, but karma? Yes, karma was a much better way for Ross to deal with everything that had gone on in his life since Maria had died.

As he thought about everything he noticed the lady standing in her doorway, the lady who had been mopping the floors in the close, the woman who had ultimately killed his father. He suddenly had an urge to thank her but knew he couldn't. How would that look to her? All he did was ask if she was ok.

"No I'm not ok, that man has just died because of me," her frail voice quivered as she spoke.

"It wasn't your fault, it was just an accident."

She had tears in her eyes as she went into her own flat and closed the door. Ross felt sorry for her.

Poor woman, he thought to himself as he closed his front door. He gazed at the picture of his Mum on the kitchen wall.

Ross felt a mix of emotions as he saw her face staring back at him. He thought about what she would say to him if she were with him at this precise moment. Knowing Maria she would have been disappointed in Ross for being so smug about what had happened.

"But you're not here are you mum and you can't say anything because you're not with me?"

He felt the sides of his eyes sting and his temples began to ache as he tried to push the emotions back into the black box he had kept inside his head for all the years Maria had been dead and even before she had died. But the black box had loosened its lid over the last few months and dark memories had reared their ugly heads, memories that had darkened Ross' outlook on life, positive reasons to go on. The memories that had been locked away for so long that they were screaming to be let out. Ross knew that there were things in his head that even he couldn't say out loud. Things that would make him sick to say and think about, things that even Maria never knew about.

Ross stared out the window as the ambulance pulled away and thought about Billy. He would be lying on a cold slab soon enough. Then he would be put into the ground and six feet of dirt would cover him, never to be seen or heard of again. Not in human form anyway.

He would forever live in Ross' mind, taunting him, making him relive every moment of torment and mental torture he had ever caused him to live through.

Ross watched until the ambulance was out of sight and he watched the people on the street go about their daily business as normal, all of them leading normal happy lives.

Ross often wondered what life would have been like if Billy had been a normal, sober Dad like the rest of the Dads in the world.

"Well Dad, what a great job you did! Well done," he said aloud. He walked into the bathroom and looked in the mirror. As he stared into his own eyes he felt the fear run through him, as if he were a child again hearing his drunken father walk through the front door. He almost heard the door slam and Billy call out drunkenly for Maria and Ross. He felt that same urge he had felt all those years ago to hide. He could hear Maria's voice echoing in his head, pleading with Billy to stop smashing things, throwing things and shouting. Ross was reliving his childhood nightmare, as he stood in his own bathroom.

He lifted his shirt and could still see the scars, the burn marks from the cigarettes. He could feel them as though they had just been put there.

Ross splashed his face with cold water. He tried to wash away the sounds in his head, the memories he had so desperately tried to keep locked away inside the box. But the lid was completely off now. As the nightmares and memories poured out he felt the anger build from his feet right to the top of his head as if he were about to explode. He closed his eyes as he remembered the cigarettes meeting his rib cage and chest, the slaps across the back of his head and neck.

Ross pulled the mirror off the wall and smashed it into the bath. There was blood on his hands and in the bath. He tried to calm himself down, trying not to be like *him*. It was just so hard to stay composed when Billy was dead but still *everywhere* Ross looked. He saw his face everywhere, in bars as men like him ogled over meaningless women who didn't care about one nighters, he saw his face in men who passed by in business suits, men who flashed their wallets at any woman who would look. He was even in the faces of women who would put it about and not think twice about who they were getting involved with.

Ross remembered that Billy had abused him too, along with Maria.

The anger boiled over as he thought about the endless nights of beatings, burns and mental abuse he had to endure. There was no way that this feeling would ever go away even though he had just watched the man who had caused his anguish die right in front of him! No amount of satisfaction would block out the last twenty odd years. If he wasn't being abused by Billy he had to listen to and watch Maria take her beating.

Ross was glad Billy was dead! But he did regret one thing, that it wasn't he who killed his Dad. He thought about that as he tried to clean his bleeding hands from the broken mirror in the bath.

Yes, it was easier for Ross that Billy had died purely by accident, that he met his maker in the old lady washing down the stairs of the close where Ross lived. However, Ross didn't feel like he had any sort of closure. Billy died only a few minutes after proclaiming his guilt and sorrow for what he had done for all those years.

That's not justice, that's a cop out, Ross thought as he washed his bloody hands under the tap. He wrapped his hands in some small hand towels and sat down on the toilet seat as he thought about everything.

How can I move on now? He was in prison for a piss easy couple of years then he gets out, gives a measly apology and then falls down a flight of stairs. What a lot of shit.

Ross squeezed the towels in his hands at the thought of Billy's easy way out. *Made your peace with God then fucked off eh Dad?*

Ross stood up and walked back to the window in the living room, the towels seeping blood. He looked out and saw a world that he could never feel a part of. He *had never* and *would never* feel happy, normal or at ease with life.

"You've just made this a whole lot fucking worse Dad."

Ross made his way into the kitchen and put some plasters on the cuts which had seemed worse at first glance but as he cleaned the blood away he saw that they were small. As he reached to put the plaster wrappings in the bin he remembered the letter that he had picked up before letting Billy in to the flat.

He walked out of the kitchen and in to the hallway and picked up the envelope. He knew exactly what it was from the stamp on the back of it, "Adoption Contact Scotland."

He hesitated for a moment, unsure what to expect from the letter. Had they found his brother?

He opened the envelope, pulled the letter out and began to read.

He read it twice to be sure that he wasn't dreaming.

Twenty Two

Lilies- flower of death

Patrick sat impatiently in the waiting room of the doctor surgery. His mind whizzed around all sorts of crazy ideas about what could be wrong with Jodie. He had never seen anything like it before. Jodie was asleep on the couch one minute and the next she was crawling along the floor, vomiting violently and screaming in terror.

When Patrick had finally managed to wake her she looked like she had no idea where she was and she was shaking so hard that Patrick had thought that she was convulsing! In all honesty he had been so terrified and had no idea what was going on he just called his out of hours practice and was told to bring her in straight away. He had insisted that he sit in with Jodie when she saw the doctor but she refused, insisting that she was fine.

The out of hours practice was deadly quiet, not like the A&E service in the Western Infirmary. The waiting room was warm and welcoming, although at that precise moment that did not compensate for the fear running through Patrick's veins. There was a radio playing quietly in the background and there was a vase filled with white lilies on the reception desk.

"Don't you think those flowers give off the wrong impression of this place?" Patrick commented with gentle sarcasm.

The receptionist glanced at the lilies then back to Patrick, "Sorry?"

"The lilies, you do know they are the flowers of death?" he smiled.

The receptionist looked away disinterested and Patrick just shrugged his shoulders and picked up the nearest magazine.

As he flicked the pages the receptionist got up and walked in to the back of the office to put some papers away. Patrick heard her return to her desk and he continued to read.

"They are quite appropriate for me," she said.

Without looking up Patrick replied, "Why's that?"

"Well, they're the flowers that were laid upon my coffin at my funeral."

The tiny hairs on the back of Patrick's neck stood on end and he looked up immediately. There she was, standing behind the reception desk as clear as he was sat in his seat, Angela Noble.

Patrick tried to stay as calm as possible and he cleared his throat and said, "They were?"

"Yes. And if you and Jodie don't get your acts together then they will be on hers too," she sounded sad, but Patrick detected a hint of anger in her tone too.

He stood up, almost defensively and walked over to the desk, "What did you say?"

The receptionist put her head round the door of the office and looked at him strangely. "I didn't say anything."

Angela was gone and the hairs were now flat on the back of his neck.

"Oh sorry, I must be hearing things," he replied.

"Although now that you mention it, you're probably right," the receptionist continued.

"About what?" Patrick answered distantly.

The receptionist looked at him a little confused. "The lilies? You said they were the flower of death."

Patrick looked down the corridor at the office door which Jodie was behind, discussing her 'episode' with her GP.

"Oh yeah, people probably won't notice anyway," he said with disregard.

The receptionist looked at Patrick, wondering what had changed in the last minute since he had mentioned the lilies. She put down a stack of papers that she had been holding and sat down on her seat.

"Are you alright sir? You seem very anxious," she asked.

116

"Yeah, I'm just worried about my fiancée that's all."

Patrick was quiet for a further few moments. What had just happened? His mind was most definitely not his own. Girls were coming in and out of his thoughts by the hour and Patrick wasn't sure if he could carry on with the invasions in his mind.

Just then the office door opened and Jodie walked down the short corridor to the waiting room. Patrick was up like a bullet from a gun and Jodie suddenly felt his grip on her waist and under arm.

"What did he say? Is it serious?" Patrick asked worriedly, quickly forgetting his encounter with the recently deceased in the doctor's waiting room.

"I'm fine, he said that it seems I have been suffering night terrors caused by stress," Jodie said expressionless.

"Night terrors? Caused by stress? What stress?" the questions were coming thick and fast.

"What do you think?" she snapped.

Patrick stood back, shocked at the sudden reaction. Jodie had never had that kind of attitude towards anyone let alone Patrick.

"Oh god I'm sorry, I don't mean to bite your head off, I'm just knackered and I wish I could relax. But I can't."

"The case, that's what's caused all of this. Why won't you just speak to me if you're feeling stressed or worried?"

"But I don't feel stressed that's the thing Patrick, I'm just tired. Exhausted actually, but I have never felt stressed to the point where I actually feel it in my gut," she sighed. "Until tonight."

They walked out to the street to get a taxi back to the apartment and Patrick recalled seeing Angela Noble stood behind the reception desk in the doctor office. It wasn't the fact that he has seen her that had bothered him, he was used to that. It was what she had *said* to him that niggled at him.

And if you and Jodie don't get your acts together then they will be on hers too.

He did not like the obvious meaning behind the words. Patrick and Jodie got in to a taxi and sat huddled together in the back. Jodie shivered due to a combination of cold and exhaustion. The roads were eerily quiet, after all it was one o'clock in the morning.

"Did the doctor prescribe anything for you?" Patrick realised he had forgotten to ask.

"Yeah I've got a prescription for some tablets to help me sleep. He said that they should also help the night terrors become less intense," she replied sleepily.

"Well, let's hope they work. Jodie, do you want me to stop working on the case? If it is causing you all this stress..."

"*No way*, those girls need your help. The police need your help."

"But..."

"We've already been through this Patrick. It's totally out of the question. Honestly I'm fine. I want you to do it and if I can be of any help then I will. God, we've been doing this for so long, I'm not about to stop the biggest investigation that you've ever had to deal with."

Patrick thought about it and she was right. But he couldn't help worrying about her. She was everything to him, the only person to ever understand every thought to go through his head, the only person to feel everything that he felt and sense every possible emotion that ran through him at any given time. They were soul mates and his love was unconditional.

"I love you Jodie, on top of everything that's what's the most important."

Jodie was fast asleep with her head on his shoulder as the taxi continued its journey back to Glasgow Harbour.

Twenty Three

Satisfaction

Satisfaction can come in many different forms, like success, achievement and happiness. In Ross' case, satisfaction had replaced happiness. In fact it hadn't replaced it as Ross had never been truly happy. Nothing in the world could make him happy, only short spells of satisfaction could get him through his life day by day, thought after thought and nightmare after nightmare.

Seeing Billy fall to his death down a flight of stairs had given Ross a short spell of satisfaction.

Murdering Angela, Rebecca and Michelle had given him three short spells of satisfaction, not one spell longer than the other. Seeing other people hurting for their loved ones because of someone else's filthy and disgraceful antics, that gave him a short spell of satisfaction. Reading of his own 'work' in the newspaper, that did it for Ross. Seeing what he had done created as a real story in a tabloid gave him that feeling too. You might also say that he *relived* his crime.

Satisfaction was becoming like a drug to Ross and unlike most of the drugs out on the Glasgow streets, not an easily accessible one!

The minute Ross did what had to be done (in his eyes) he felt the satisfaction flow slowly through his body. It warmed his skin, his blood and bones. It reached in to his heart as though his heart required it to be able to fulfil its purpose. He felt like the satisfaction was slowly building him back in to a state that could cope with all the bad luck that life had thrown at him.

He thought about Jeffery, what kind of life was he living? Did he know that he had been adopted? Did he even care? Ross did. He cared that this Jeffery fellow had been given a lucky escape. He had been given the chance of a normal life, a normal childhood without blackened memories.

Ross thought about his own life, thought about his trail of bad luck and how he seemed to be the debris from the abusive life his father had forced him to live in.

Some people live to work, some people work to live, some people live for the thrill. Then there are those who live for the simple things like marriage, children and mortgages. Some people live to travel the world and explore different cultures and ways of life.

For Ross there was now the slow and painful realisation that the satisfaction was keeping him from killing himself, that it was keeping him alive and at the moment it was barely doing that.

A fix, that's what I need, to keep going, to get justice and stay sane and to feel alive, Ross thought to himself.

Short spells of satisfaction...

Ross made his plan. A plan that was going to destroy lives, cause destruction and chaos for the people involved but mostly, give him the satisfaction that he needed to stay sane.

Twenty Four

Someone in the shadows

Patrick watched Mark as he worked behind the bar of, The Blue Bar, the evening after Jodie's night terror. As he watched he saw an endless flow of women flirting with Mark, some discreetly and some not so discreetly!

Mark didn't even have to do much to get the attention he wanted, by the looks of things all he had to do was say, "What would you like?" or, "What can I get you?"

Patrick laughed when one woman actually told him what *she* could do for *him*. As they served together Patrick began to feel the pressure lift from the past few days, Jodie becoming ill, in a sense and the appearance of Angela. The thought of planning experiments to carry out to try and come up with some solutions that may take the case forward was resting quietly at the back of his mind as he served cocktails and chatted to Mark about general things.

"How do you do that?" Patrick asked Mark after yet another woman passed her number over with her money.

"What?" Mark asked sheepishly.

"That! Women are literally throwing themselves at you."

Mark laughed as he unloaded the clean glasses from the compact industrial dishwasher beneath the till, "Literally? Now that would be something I'd like to watch!"

"You know what I mean. Are you actually going to call any of them?" Patrick asked.

Mark took the bundle of phone numbers from his back pocket and smiled, "Probably not mate, not really that interested to be honest."

He put the little pieces of paper back in his pocket and continued unloading the dishwasher. "What about you?" Mark asked.

"What about me?"

"You don't fancy any of those women? Some of them are alright!" he winked.

"You know I don't, I mean yeah some of them are quite nice, but I am engaged."

"Just testing you Patrick, from what I've seen of you two it seems you are pretty set on each other!" Mark kept his head in his task as he spoke.

What Mark said made Patrick doubt that for just a moment. *What if this case is pushing Jodie away? What if she is not ok with all of this? But she said so!* he questioned himself.

Mark looked on, wondering why he seemed so distant all of a sudden. "You alright?"

Patrick snapped back from his thoughts at Mark's voice. "Yes, sorry I was miles away. Are those glasses ready then?"

Patrick took the glasses and began placing them back on the shelf behind him. Jodie was in his mind once more. He had to admit the knot in his stomach was becoming tighter the more he recalled the terrors and he couldn't imagine how she was feeling about it all. As he stacked the glasses and became entangled in his thoughts, he went over the experiments that he would be carrying out the next day with D.S Preston and D.C Lang. He would be conducting these in the homes of the victims and any other related places that were necessary to the murder cases. He was feeling strangely nervous about it.

The nervousness must have presented itself in his expression because Mark asked him again, "Patrick, are you sure you're alright? You seem really down about something?"

Patrick regarded this and took the opportunity to get things off his chest. "Not really actually, can I trust that you'll keep this to yourself if I tell you?" Patrick sincerely hoped that he could.

"Of course you can trust me, who am I going to tell?" Mark's smile was genuine, understanding that Patrick felt relief for seeing it.

"Well, you know Jodie? We're going through a bit of a tough time just now..."

"Relationship stuff?" Mark jumped in.

Patrick shook his head. "No, nothing like that, but I'm scared that it might come between us."

Mark looked on at Patrick and he could see that the poor guy was genuinely struggling to keep his stress under control as he spoke.

"What is it Patrick, honestly you can trust me?" he placed a friendly hand on Patrick's shoulder.

Patrick knew that Preston and Lang would be livid with him for breaking their discretion, especially if the media were to get wind of their arrangement, but for some reason he really felt like he could trust Mark.

"Have you seen the news and the papers over the last few months?"

"Here and there, I don't really pay much attention to the news to be honest. I know that makes me sound a bit ignorant!" Mark replied.

"So you haven't heard about the girls that were killed in the city centre?"

"No. What has that got to do with you and Jodie? Don't tell me you're the killer?" Mark laughed as he spoke.

"Very funny, if only it was as simple as that!"

"Ok now I'm lost."

"I'm a psychic medium Mark. I run the West End Spiritualist Church with Jodie."

Mark seemed a little shocked, not to Patrick's surprise since he had grown up with people looking at him like he was crazy.

"You're a psychic?" Mark's face had changed expression from concern to shock.

"Yes. Do you believe in it?"

Mark shook his head. "It has never been proven to me. I've wanted to believe in it for a long time but never have I been shown that I should."

"Well what I am about to tell you may or may not make you change your mind."

"Ok, I am listening."

As Patrick told Mark everything that was going on, Mark listened intently. He couldn't quite believe what he was hearing but he knew that Patrick spoke words of truth, truth that was chilling to him.

"So you're telling me that you are working with the police to try to find the person who killed these girls?"

"Yep and it seems to be affecting Jodie a hell of a lot more than it is me and I don't know why."

"Do you think that maybe it is because she is worried about it affecting you and the stress of it all is just getting to her?"

"Yeah, but it all came on so suddenly. She seems really ill because of it. I'm really worried about her." Patrick suddenly felt himself begin to well up. He tried to compose himself and took a deep breath. "I suppose I'm just going to have to work really hard to solve this case so we can go back to our normal lives."

Mark looked at Patrick and saw the worry in his eyes. *He must really love her*, he thought to himself as he patted him on the back. "Couldn't you just tell the police that you can't do it anymore as it's affecting your personal life?" he asked.

"No way, I can't let these girls down now. I've not even really started yet."

"What do you mean?" Mark wondered.

"Well, I still need to carry out some experiments and séances to see if I can get some vital information that will lead the police to the arrest of the person who did this."

Mark was silent for a while. He ran over the large amount of information he had just received in his head and tried to piece it together.

"What's wrong? You think I am mad don't you?" Patrick spoke the words he had so many times before.

"Not at all, I believe you."

"Really?"

"Why would you lie? It's a lot to deal with Patrick. I'm sorry for your troubles. If you need any help with anything, even just someone to talk to, I can be that person." Mark sounded sincere.

"Thanks Mark. Thanks for listening and not judging."

Unbeknown to Patrick, Mark was not the only person who had been listening.

Twenty Five

A grave message

The flat was in complete darkness on his arrival home from his shift. Not only was there darkness, but silence too, an eerily chilling silence. Something was wrong, but what? He switched on the hall light and it shone into the living room. For some reason he felt frozen to the spot. Where was Jodie? What was this feeling of ice, deep within him?

"Jodie, are you there?"

Nothing...

A shadow crossed the doorway of the living room. If it hadn't been for the light from the hall then he may not have seen it.

"Jodie..."

Then came the feeling of goose bumps, not from the cold, but from the chill deep within *himself*. There was a feeling of uncertainty around him, he felt like he should know even though he *didn't* know what was about to happen, but he knew for sure that something was building. He took a step forward, to be met with a flicker of the light bulb above him.

A warning?

He inhaled deeply, almost silently so he could listen for something, anything.

Patrick couldn't decide why he felt so scared, he had dealt with this since he was a young child. It wasn't like he was watching a horror movie, but he did have the feeling of terror that a horror movie would give you if you were secretly watching as a child. You knew you weren't allowed to watch it but you were so curious as to why not, the fear of the movie itself and the fear that your parents would catch you watching it was enough to lure you in.

Patrick knew he should walk straight into his living room and confront the situation but he was scared as he didn't know what he was confronting. Was it human or spirit? Was that why he was scared, because he wasn't sure?

He decided to bite the bullet and confront whatever was in his home. He walked straight into the living room and to his relief, he saw Jodie standing by the sliding glass doors with one hand pressed against the glass. They were partially open and the night breeze swirled around the room.

"Why didn't you answer me when I called out?" he asked, feeling slightly annoyed and a little relieved.

"Why haven't *you*?"

"What?" he replied feeling puzzled. Then something inside him clicked. That was it, that horrible chilling feeling was back and it was colder than before.

Jodie was stood there but it was not Jodie who spoke. The figure turned and the blue lips almost glowed in the light from the hallway. The eyes were dark and lifeless and the voice was haunting, definitely not Jodie's. He looked passed the woman and saw a cool mist lingering where her hand had been just a moment before.

Patrick drew back in fear. "What do you mean?" He managed to gather himself and took a stance that showed bravery.

"It's *there*," the voice muffled now.

"What is? Tell me!" Patrick almost shouted now.

"You can't see. You've been blinded but you must see," the voice was distressed.

"Must see what? I can't do this by myself."

It was Rebecca's voice which came from Jodie, but almost as soon as she spoke she was gone. Jodie's body collapsed to the floor and Patrick ran to her.

"Jodie, wake up!"

Jodie opened her eyes and she looked at Patrick who now had tears in his own eyes. She took his face in her hands and he helped her up.

"What the hell is going on?" he said.

"You tell me. I wake up on the floor and you've got tears in your eyes hovering over me," her voice shook.

Jodie's worry became more intense. Patrick helped her over to the couch and they sat down. Jodie steadied herself.

"Right, that's it. I think we need to get away for a while."

"What good will that do?" She asked as he held her close to his chest.

Another episode, what is happening to me?

Patrick knew what good it would do for them, for Jodie, to get away from the stress and uncertainty of the case. He also considered what bad would come of him abandoning it for a few days. Would Preston and Lang even allow it?

Surely a few days won't change much? He thought.

"Give me a few days to get it sorted. We need to get away from all of this. I'm sick of seeing you so messed up. You're definitely picking up the spirits and I don't like it. It's not good for you."

"*You* don't like it? I can't stand it, Patrick I can barely remember afterwards, all I know is that I feel like I'm going mad."

"I know. I'll speak to Preston and Lang and I'll try to get them a few things to work with and then we can leave for a few days. I'm putting you first Jodie, I'm going to take care of you."

Jodie shivered in his arms as he held her, comforted her. Patrick had to try and help lead the police to solving this case sooner than he had thought.

You can't see. You've been blinded but you must see, he repeated it in his head. *What the hell does that mean?*

***

Ross sat in his kitchen staring at the newspaper cuttings and pictures that he had of Rebecca, Angela and Michelle. He thought about their deaths and how much they were deserving of it. He remembered about the conversation he had heard earlier that evening. Psychic medium was he?

Seems I have something of a challenge on my hands, we'll see about that Mr Psychic won't we?

He held a picture of Patrick and Jodie he had found in a local newspaper advertising the spiritualist church and its services.

Jodie, was the last name in his mind before he fell asleep.

Twenty Six

The purpose of existence

When the soul leaves the body, it doesn't leave the body looking like a human does. It's almost like a mist hovering over what once was its home, the body. If the soul passes gently, naturally, then it settles on another plane, the spirit plane as I am sure you are aware of.

However, if the soul is forced from the human form then usually the soul does not settle straight away. It becomes lost between the earth plane and spirit plane, often not knowing that they have passed. Other times, the spirit is fully aware that they have passed on to a new level of existence and they have ends that need tying up before they can move on.

This was the case for Angela Noble, Michelle Levine and Rebecca Collins. Their souls were forced from their bodies, unwilling to leave. They were forced to leave in such a violent manner, forced to endure pain and fear, terror and desperation being the last human emotions to be experienced.

All of the spirits had unfinished business that could not wait, that business being Ross Turner, the one who forced their souls from their bodies, the one who took their lives in his hands and turned his own life's miseries into an act of violence that caused misery for their families.

Angela Noble's energy was the strongest of the spirits, as she was the one who was murdered first, her spirit had had time to adjust to its new existence and ability to communicate. Angela was spending her new found existence working her energy on Patrick, keeping her own spirit calm to try to lead him to the murderer. But for some reason his ability to pick up her spiritual connection was not working one hundred percent. She would explain everything in detail to Patrick a million times over each day she was in 'limbo' but he was not picking up on it. He would only hear certain things, see her at certain times.

Even Michelle had tried to contact him, using a more forceful energy, but even that did not work. Michelle Levine's spirit did have a strong energy, but she chose to not to make too much contact until absolutely necessary. She chose to use her energy for the purpose of revenge. She was an angry spirit, and being angry sucked up all of her energy quickly, so she decided to keep it stored and use it for her only purpose of existence now. She was angry for becoming only an existence now, she had had plans for life, a future. Her human form had been studying law at university. She had dreamed of becoming a successful lawyer and providing a life for herself. But it had been snatched away from her in an instant, by a monster, a monster who claimed grief in his own mind as an excuse to commit these acts of murder. How dare he take away her future? Who was he to make the decision that she deserved to die? Michelle knew that her soul and spirit could not rest until Ross Turner was either behind bars or dead!

Rebecca Collins was the newest spirit, having been last to fall into the fateful hands of Ross, she had been ripped from her body so quickly that she hadn't realised that she was dead for three days. She had been at home for those three days, wondering why she was feeling a sense of loneliness and despair. It was then that she remembered the headache, the running, the alley. She remembered every moment of what had happened and even though it was not possible, it made her feel sick to her stomach. Rebecca had become an existence alongside Angela and Michelle. She had wanted to move on to the spirit plane immediately after meeting them, but she couldn't. Their spirits had become one, full of purpose that should be served no matter how long it would take.

In death, there is no time but only existence. Angela had to remind the other spirits how long it had been for them. The longer the spirits were together, the angrier Michelle became and loneliness became overwhelming for Rebecca, however she could cope better with the feelings than Michelle. Angela took on the role of the messenger within the spirits.

But as existence went on, the harder it was becoming to break the barrier that Patrick's mind had created. Nothing she did would penetrate that barrier and there were a few times where Angela wanted to give up but continued with her attempts. It was then that Jodie had entered the equation. Angela realised that Jodie's mind would be open to all of the spirits and even more so because she was also a psychic medium.

Jodie's mind was full of anxiety which made her vulnerable to the energies of Angela, Michelle and Rebecca. This meaning that Jodie's mind could be harmed if not treated gently by them. But Angela knew that Jodie was their only hope of successfully revealing Ross and having him put to prison for their deaths.

Angela would try absolutely everything in her power to show Jodie everything that had happened and everything that she could foresee. Being able to see the future was a gift that the other spirits did not have, so it was down to Angela to make every attempt to contact Jodie and help her lead Patrick to the killer before it was too late. The spirits were with Patrick and Jodie every minute of every day in human time, awake or asleep, in their dreams and in their minds. Jodie was seeing much more than Patrick was but she wasn't speaking in full about her visions. Jodie was terrified of what she was seeing but still only spoke in small snippets to Patrick.

But even though Jodie was being shown what had happened to the girls and events that may occur if time went on without justice, something else was blocking Jodie's ability to see the truth.

Twenty Seven

Mirror image

The photographs and newspaper cuttings were beginning to take up a lot of space on the small wall at the back of the bedroom. The room was barely slept in and used more as a storage room, storage of reminders of the ill fated deaths, reminders that were put there to keep the mind on track.

Maria's face, Angela, Michelle and Rebecca's faces, even Billy's face, they all stared out at Ross as he studied them. He looked into his mothers eyes and the grief was overbearing. It tugged at his gut as he felt sick with emotion, anger at Billy, disgust at the girls. But he felt something else too, something that made him, for the first time question whether he should carry on or not. Was it doubt that he would be found out too soon? Maybe he should lay off for a while?

The thought of not carrying on made Ross' head hurt. He had to continue, had to go on. Maria's death could not be in vain, something good had to come from the pain of losing her. Ross moved his eyes across the space covering the wall on to another face. Billy, now dead and for a short while this made the gut wrenching feeling about his mothers pain go away, but it came back like it always did. The pain would only remove itself from Ross' heart for short periods of time, after death, but without a shadow of a doubt it would present itself again, stabbing at him like a freshly sharpened knife.

Applying his pain to those who Ross saw partly responsible for his mother's death was the only thing that could get him through his never ending grief.

He quickly moved his eyes away from Billy, no longer being able to take the image in his head of his dysfunctional family and moved on to the girls. Those three faces stared back at him, smiling innocently, dressed in their alluring attire, as if getting ready to possibly ruin an unsuspecting happy family.

Any pain Ross had been feeling diminished very slightly as he looked at their faces, knowing that he had rid the world of a family disaster waiting to happen. But the pain didn't leave entirely, as he knew that there were many more out there that he had to deal with.

He smiled at the girls photos as his eyes left them and moved over the newspaper report cuttings and on to two newer additions to the wall. His smile diminished as he looked into the eyes of the new faces. The new faces had become obstacles for Ross. Obstacles create problems and problems slow down the process of revenge.

Ross read the cutting he had found in the local paper about the West End Spiritualist Church; West End Spiritualist church invites you along to witness the connection between life and spirit. If you are looking for a connection with a passed loved one, answers to questions that nobody else can answer, or just curious about our spiritual abilities then come along to one of our demonstrations. You'll be amazed by what our mediums can do for you. Anyone who attends will be welcomed warmly and safely by a number of our mediums, all of which have a blend of unique abilities that will connect to the spirit world for you. Come and meet the head of our church Patrick McLaughlin and his fiancée Jodie Jenkins who will be able to comfort you with a private message, or simply be part of a demonstration where you may be lucky enough to receive a reading. We are open Monday 8pm to 10pm, Wednesday 8pm to 10pm or Sunday 12pm to 4pm.

He looked at their faces and thought about the realisation of which Patrick and Jodie were. They were resources for the Police and obstacles for Ross. But maybe he could switch that around.

Maybe the obstacles could become *part* of the revenge? Maybe the obstacles don't have to be obstacles at all? Maybe Ross could use the new faces as his resource in his plans.

"So much for being psychic," Ross smiled. "You haven't even figured me out yet!"

He walked out from the bedroom and closed the door quietly behind him, almost as if he didn't want the faces in the photos to hear him leave the room. He made his way into the bathroom and as he looked into the cracked and damaged mirror he wondered if Patrick would be able to figure it out before Ross could make his move.

Well, it has been almost three months and he hasn't figured it out so far.

This made Ross smile and he enjoyed knowing that he was still a black silhouette to Patrick and the Police.

He crouched down and pulled the side panel of the bath away from the tub and reached under. He gripped his hand around a plastic waterproof bag and slid it out from underneath the bath tub. As he unzipped it he pictured the possibility of Patrick knocking on his door. He felt his adrenaline kick in at the thought that it could all stop at any given time but knowing that it was unlikely at this moment. It hadn't happened so far, so why now?

He put his hand into the bag and pulled out a plastic supermarket bag and emptied the contents.

A male (very realistic) styled hair piece, which was dark in colour and shorter than his own hair, a large bottle of professional skin enhancer, and several small cases containing blue contact lenses and a hair net. He also brought out of the bag a very small case containing dentures and a pair of designer glasses, slim frames with rectangular lenses.

There was also an envelope in the bag containing two photographs, one of himself and one of another man. The last thing to come out of the never ending bag was an extendable mirror. He had bought it to replace the one he had smashed into the bath after Billy had died. He stood up and placed the mirror onto the edge of the small windowsill. He looked at his reflection whilst he held the photo of the second man up against his face.

"The only thing that can't be changed is the voice," Ross spoke in to the mirror.

"Everything else is perfect, we don't look anything like each other!"

Ross began to apply the products to himself. He watched as the transformation in the small mirror took place. He placed the contact lenses into his eyes carefully and not without difficulty. It was not that he struggled to get them into place, he hated the feeling of touching his own eye, however he knew that everything that he was doing was absolutely necessary for his gain.

"Let's see if Mr McLaughlin can use his psychic abilities to piece together this part of the puzzle," he said as he adjusted the hair piece and set the artificial teeth in place.

The man in the second photograph and staring back at Ross from the mirror was Mark.

Twenty Eight

Experimental investigations

"Automatic writing?" Lang asked as Patrick laid out his equipment on the desk in Angela Noble's bedroom.

"Yes Jim, automatic writing," Patrick replied.

Paul Preston and Jim Lang had arranged for them and Patrick to visit the homes of the victims and have Patrick conduct some experiments to see if they could come up with anything that could help the police in their investigations. At first the families of the girls were a little reluctant but with some encouragement and reassurance from Patrick they were able to access some personal belongings of the girls and he was able to come up with some experiments to get the information that they had all hoped for.

"I can assure you Mrs Noble, I am genuine. I sincerely believe that I can help this case, I can get justice for your daughter," Patrick had said to Angela's mother.

Mrs Noble had been clutching a scarf that Angela had been wearing on the night before she was murdered when she was discussing the process with Patrick.

"If you give me permission to do this then I will require some of Angela's personal belongings, like some clothing, perhaps something from the night before it happened?"

"Yes that's ok. I can give you this!" Mrs Noble's voice was fragile, cracking in between words as she held up the scarf, "She was wearing this the last time I saw her."

"That would be extremely helpful Mrs Noble thank you and I promise to return all of the items I use and keep you well informed of anything that I find out from the experiments."

Lang watched as Patrick arranged everything he needed for the experiment and felt completely out of the loop. "So, what exactly is it that you are doing?"

Patrick sat down at the small desk in Angela's room and the scarf lay across it, "I am going to ask some questions in my head and if I get any reply then my message will be conveyed on a piece of paper."

"You mean you will write it down?" Preston asked.

"No, she will," Patrick said.

"How is that possible?" Lang asked.

Patrick was slowly beginning to lose his patience. "Right, remember how this all came about? I came to you, gave you my story, you both chose to allow me to work with you and then I gave you that reading Jim?" he paused as Lang met his gaze, "so how is it possible? Because I am a psychic medium Jim, it's my ability and I use it."

Preston rolled his eyes. "I thought you two were past this?"

"We are, I was only asking." Lang said defensively.

"Well ask yourself how I knew what I did when I gave you that reading!"

Lang said nothing as Patrick pulled out his large note pad and a pen. Preston put an arm on Patrick's shoulder, knowing something wasn't right. "You ok Patrick? You seem very tense today."

Patrick realised how tense his shoulders were and he allowed them to slump, "I am tense. It's Jodie, she isn't very well. The doctor says it is stress and I think it is due to all of this."

"I wasn't taking the piss Patrick, I genuinely didn't know what automatic writing was." Lang said.

"I know, sorry for snapping at you. I shouldn't be getting stressed just before I'm about to do this or it won't work properly."

Lang nodded in understanding, out of all the people in the world he knew how difficult it was to work under stress when there were personal problems going on.

"Why would she be so stressed about your work?" Preston asked.

"She is worried about me taking part in the case and she is having terrible anxiety attacks at really random times. She has been prescribed sleeping pills."

"Sleeping pills?" Preston considered this. "Well, a few nights proper sleep and I am sure that she will be back to her normal self." Preston could see that Patrick did not believe this to be the truth and honestly he knew that his words did not offer any comfort to Patrick.

"No, I don't think that the sleeping pills will settle her anxiety attacks."

"Why not?" Lang asked

"Because I think that the spirits of the girls are trying to communicate with me through her and for some reason I can't pick up the messages. It's causing the spirits to torment Jodie's mental well-being."

Preston and Lang looked at Patrick feeling a little stunned. Lang was beginning to feel a little nervous now about the experiment which was about to commence.

"Look, you said getting yourself stressed out before an experiment may cause it to fail. Why don't we get on with the job in hand and then we can continue this discussion after we have finished." Lang made it sound like a question but his words were firm.

This was a serious murder inquiry and he couldn't help but feel like he was starring in a badly produced low budget film. The police had scanned hours of CCTV footage from the bars that the girls were all last seen in and footage from the various street cameras and to their frustration had found absolutely nothing that they could lead with. There had been no lead on the DNA samples that had been carried out after Rebecca's murder. Not so much as a hair had been found on any of the girls clothing. The case was at a standstill and Lang knew fine well that the public were not safe from the person who was responsible for the killings. He often thought to himself that maybe the murderer was a ghost seeing as there was nothing to lead the case a step further.

Now he found himself in the bedroom of one of the victims, looking at various personal belongings on a table and talking to Patrick about his fiancée and her sleeping problems. Lang knew now that the spirit world was real, Patrick had proved this to him, but he still could not help but feel like all of this experiment stuff was just a little bit ridiculous.

"Yes, you're right Lang, I need to focus. Could you switch out the light please?" Patrick motioned to the switch next to the bedroom door.

Lang switched out the light. *Oh for god sake! Does the room really have to be in darkness?*

Lang and Preston sat down on Angela Nobles bed as Patrick placed his pen to the paper, not in a way that he was ready to take notes with his pen at the top left hand side of the page, but directly in the middle. Patrick did not apply pressure as he did this but instead held the pen so gently that if he were to attempt to write with this pressure then it would not be possible.

"Now what?" Lang whispered to Preston.

"We wait, and we wait in silence," Preston replied sternly. The room was still, silent, like it was on a television screen and the viewer had pressed pause.

"Angela, I'm here to help you. I am open to your spiritual presence," Patrick spoke quietly and slowly.

Lang felt laughter rise from his stomach but he kept it in as he listened.

"I feel your presence please give me your message."

This is pointless, there is no way that a ghost is going to move that pen and actually write something on that piece of paper, Lang thought to himself.

The silence somehow managed to deepen within the room. It sank into the darkness, the silence and darkness becoming one. A few more moments passed as Patrick sat with the pen resting gently on the paper.

Preston sat completely still, his eyes never leaving Patrick. Lang's mind would have wandered by now in any other situation where he would have to stay silently still for this period of time, but not now.

Now, the pen moved, slowly and in judder like movements across the page. Patrick's eyes were closed now and as Lang watched intensely, he could see that every single hair on Patricks arm stood on end, perfectly straight. Patrick's hand moved in small circular movements, quick at times. To Preston and Lang it looked as if Patrick were just making shapes. They were yet to see the words that Angela had written.

Twenty Nine

A black mist

"Time is running out," Preston read this from the piece of paper.

"Do not listen to them," Lang read aloud too.

Patrick tried to make sense of the random words and sentences on the paper but he just couldn't understand them.

"Don't listen to who?" Lang continued.

"I have not got a clue Jim. Honestly... I'm stumped." Patrick shook his head in frustration.

Patrick took the paper from Preston and looked at it feeling dumbfounded.

Time is running out for what? He thought to himself. *Time is running out for who?*

The men stood in Angela Nobles bedroom for sometime after Patrick had concluded the experiment. All three men were feeling completely lost with everything about the case.

The words on the paper were scattered, none of which had any kind of ability to make sense of the murders.

Preston cleared his throat. "You said that you wanted to talk to us about Jodie?"

"Yes I did. I think I am going to take her away for a bit. She needs some time to get her head together, we both do."

"Do you think that is a wise move, we're in the middle of a triple murder inquiry?" Lang sounded annoyed.

Patrick looked dead into his eyes. "Yes Jim, a murder inquiry that is at a complete stand still."

Silence filled the room for a few moments before Preston spoke out. "Look, I think it is safe to say that we all need a bit of a breather from this. Lets go for a coffee and then we can discuss it further. I don't think that we should talk about this here, out of respect."

Patrick cleared away the equipment that he was using during the experiment and left the room to hand back Angela's scarf to Mrs Noble.

"Paul, this is not working," Lang said when Patrick was out of the room.

"What do you mean?" Preston asked.

"This whole medium thing, it's just not working. I mean, do you think this is getting us any further?"

Preston regarded Lang's comment. Was it working having Patrick on the case? He really wanted to believe that it was. But for whatever reason, Patrick just wasn't coming up with anything that Preston and Lang could investigate, but then, neither were they.

Maybe Lang had been right. But then how would Lang explain his reading? Research?

"All of this is giving me a headache. Let's call it a day and go for that coffee," Preston said.

"Fine, but this is not going to go away, we have to make a decision," Lang replied bluntly. They left Angela Nobles room and went down stairs into the living room, where they found Patrick comforting Mrs Noble.

The living room was decorated a teal blue colour, with a large glass lampshade hanging from the ceiling. There were several photo frames in different parts of the room all containing family photographs, all of which contained Angela either hugging another person or posing for the camera. There were a few of her in a graduation gown too.

Mrs Noble had been crying when Preston and Lang were upstairs and when they appeared in the room below, Preston was surprised to see that every single photo frame was lying on the floor.

Mrs Noble was no longer crying but instead she stared at each one, all face down on the brown shag pile carpet. Her expression was one of shock with a hint of a smile, but only noticeable if one were to be looking for a smile.

"What happened here? Are you alright Mrs Noble?" It was Lang who spoke.

"I came down to hand back the belongings and all I could hear was banging, it was light but they were coming fast," Patrick said.

Lang looked up and could see that the bulb was missing from the glass shade hanging down from the ceiling. He moved his eyes down to see if he could place the bulb, only to find it smashed on the carpet.

"It was Angela, my girl. She was here," Mrs Noble said in a small trembling voice.

"What?" Preston felt disbelief.

"Did you witness this?" Lang asked Patrick.

"Yes, I walked in to see what the noise was and Mrs Noble was standing in corner of the room watching the frames falling over. The bulb smashed in its place in the shade and the glass fluttered down, almost like a feather." Even Patrick sounded stunned by the happenings.

"I think we should get this cleaned up," Preston walked over to Mrs Noble, still standing in the corner of the room, still staring at the frames on the floor. "Mrs Noble, I think we should clear up the glass," he took her gently by the arm.

Preston led Mrs Noble out of the room and Patrick looked around the room, as if he were looking for anything else that may be out of place.

"What has *actually* happened here?" Lang almost whispered.

"Angela's spirit didn't fully leave our presence by the looks of it, seems as if she wanted her mum to know that she is still here." Patrick said.

"Uh cut the crap Patrick, you sure she hasn't just gone nuts?"

"How the hell can you be so insensitive? Would you say that if it was your dad?" Patrick snapped back.

"Don't you dare bring my personal stuff into this Patrick, all I am saying is this all looks a little staged."

Patrick couldn't quite believe that Lang was saying this, how could he think such a thing? "Tell me, what would she get out of doing something like this? I mean really, she would only be lying to herself. And anyway, I saw it happen."

"Did you?"

"Oh so you think I'm lying now? So what's the point in me being here then if that's the case?" Patrick was beginning to lose his temper just as Preston returned with a dustpan and brush.

"What is the problem here?" Preston said as he closed the door behind him.

"Ask your colleague here, I'm going to wait in the car," Patrick replied. "Is Mrs Noble ok?" he asked just before leaving.

"Yeah, she is fine, she is having a cigarette at the back door," Preston replied as he bent down to sweep up the glass from the bulb.

Patrick nodded in satisfaction at the answer and left the house, he couldn't bare to be around Lang another minute, he was being so unreasonable at the current situation and it was all Patrick could do not to punch him in the mouth.

As he waited in the car outside, he thought about Angela. He rewound his memory to when Mrs Noble was stood in the corner of the room watching the frames falling to the carpet, one by one. She watched as if she were watching somebody make their way around her living room knocking the frames down.

That's what Patrick had done. He watched Angela knock the frames down, not in anger, but in desperation. She was trying desperately to tell the people who were alive and around her, who they were looking for. Not just Angela but Rebecca and Michelle were too. However the eyes of those who needed to see were clouded by the black mist that emanated from that *one* person that nobody had uncovered yet.

All the while, Patrick was being stared in the face by that black mist, every moment, every blink of the eye, every word exchanged, that mist was getting thicker and nobody could see through it!

Thirty

Taking a break

The short car journey to the cafe was silent. Preston felt like the situation had to be cooled off before any conversation took place. Lang didn't know what to say to either Preston or Patrick, mainly because he knew that Patrick was a genuine medium, which annoyed him because up until recent events he hadn't believed in spirits at all. Now he felt like he had been forced to believe it, after all it was proven to him on a personal note, but for some reason unknown to him, Patrick hadn't come up with anything sufficient to work on.

Patrick was just too angry to speak to anyone in case he said something he would regret. He was so angry at Lang's attitude towards him and his involvement in the case, he was trying his best to get as much spiritual evidence as he could for those girls and all Lang could do was criticize and make snide comments.

The car pulled up outside a small cafe on Hyndland Road, near the centre of the West End. It was early afternoon by now and there was a break in the clouds as the sun shone through. There were little steel tables and chairs neatly arranged outside the cafe and the smell of fresh coffee and bread seemed to relax them as they got out of the car.

"You two go in and order, I'll grab us a table, I need a cigarette," Patrick said.

"Do you want a coffee?" Lang asked.

Patrick almost didn't want to answer him, he still felt so angry. "Yes please," he replied through gritted teeth.

As Preston and Lang were inside ordering their coffee's Patrick lit his cigarette and he instantly felt the nicotine spread through his veins, calming him. He knew that it was a psychological thing to *feel* the nicotine calming his nerves and his anger, but for now he would enjoy that feeling. As he drew on the tip, he watched the bustle of Hyndland Road pass him by. He watched people going about their daily routines, picking up groceries, meeting friends.... enjoying simple carefree days. Patrick couldn't remember what it was like to have carefree days. He watched every male figure that passed him. He pictured each one of them as the black silhouette in his dream.

He could be anyone, anywhere.

Why can I not figure this out? He was shouting inwardly as he searched his mind for anything that would help switch the bulb on in his head.

Preston and Lang appeared at the table with a tray of hot coffees and some shortbread. They sat down and for a few moments the only thing that passed their lips was the coffee and shortbread.

"Patrick, I'm sorry for acting like..."

"An arse?" Patrick abruptly finished Lang's sentence for him.

"Easy, I was going to say for acting like an idiot," Lang replied.

"I think we should use Patrick's word," Preston laughed as he blew in to his coffee, which broke the tension.

"I really am sorry though, I think we all got a little stressed out back there, not being able to figure out those messages and then seeing all of those picture frames being scattered everywhere. I suppose I freaked out a bit," Lang said.

"Finally, you admit that it scares you," Patrick said triumphantly.

"Is that what the problem has been with you two all of this time? Jim's a big girl's blouse?" Preston was laughing loudly now.

"Aye, alright let's not get carried away here, let's just get to the point of why we're having this coffee break. Patrick you wanted to talk to us more about Jodie?" Lang was desperately but modestly trying to shift the subject on to something else.

Patrick and Preston carried on laughing for a few more moments which happened to relax them all. It had been a frustrating day and Lang's fear had broken the tension, much to his annoyance. Patrick and Preston composed themselves, allowing the laughter to subside while Lang sat quietly, waiting for the joke at his expense to be over.

"Ok," Patrick took a breath. "I was actually going to ask if I could take a week or so off from the case."

"You want to take time off now?" Preston asked, any trace of smile had now left him.

"Yes now. I need to take Jodie away from this for a while. Help her to clear her head, calm herself down." Patrick understood Preston's frustration but was firm with his words.

"I think that would be the best thing for all of us to be honest," Lang said.

Patrick looked at Lang, shocked at his words. "You agree with me?"

"Yes as a matter of fact I do. We all know that the lack of evidence on our side of the case is not looking good and you said yourself that stress can stop your senses from working properly. If Jodie is having problems, then obviously it is going to have an affect on you."

What Lang said was completely true, Patrick just couldn't believe that he was the one saying it instead of Preston.

"I've got to say I'm a little surprised that you are the one that is supporting me on this."

"Well, if you go away for a while, then come back with a clear head maybe you will actually come up with something feasible that we can investigate further," Lang said.

"No offence meant, I'm presuming?" Patrick raised one eyebrow.

"Not at all, you said yourself that you were stumped by those messages back at the Nobles household."

"I was. I still am. But I'm sure that I will be able to find something, even if it is just a small thing, to work with. I am sure I can help catch this guy. I just need a week to rest my mind and help Jodie to rest hers."

Preston was quiet for a while. He listened to Patrick as he talked about where he was taking Jodie and how he was going to look after her.

"How did you manage to get a cottage in Loch Lomond?" Lang asked.

"My great Auntie owned it, left it to my Mum when she died. It's the perfect getaway, it overlooks the loch and it has a huge garden with decking and a built in barbecue."

"A cottage, you sure it's not a *mansion* overlooking the loch?" Lang laughed.

"I know. I don't know why we don't use it more often. When this is all over, you two should come down and see it."

As they finished their drinks and paid the bill, Preston finally spoke, "As long as it will be no more than a week. I understand that you have things that you need to sort out, but so do we. We have a murderer on the loose, I just want to catch him before someone else is killed."

Patrick suddenly felt guilty, he felt like he was abandoning everything to go on holiday.

"It's not as if it's a five star luxury cruise I'm leaving for, I will definitely be back in a week, I promise."

Preston knew that he couldn't force Patrick to stay. It wasn't as if he was an actual police officer or getting paid for what he was doing. As far as the press were concerned it was a police matter and that was all there was too it. Although, Preston felt uneasy about letting Patrick walk out at this particular moment he knew there was pretty much nothing he could do about it. He knew that because of the lack of physical evidence and witnesses to the murders of Angela, Rebecca and Michelle, that unless Patrick worked it out spiritually, the case had absolutely no chance of justice.

"I know you will. I hope a Jodie gets better," Preston said, but he kept his thoughts to himself.

Thirty One

A close friend

As Patrick opened the door he heard Jodie talking to someone. She was speaking quietly and in short sentences, almost like she was speaking with someone she was not supposed to. "I don't know what to do," she said, almost whispering.

Patrick made his way into the kitchen, where he could hear her voice. As he opened the door, he was surprised to see Mark standing there.

"What are you doing here?" Patrick said, failing to hide the surprise in his tone.

"Hi Patrick, I bumped into Jodie in town earlier when I was out and she asked me back."

Patrick was happy that she hadn't been alone all day, having someone to talk to would have helped take her mind off things.

"You don't know what to do about what?" Patrick asked Jodie.

"About the sleeping pills, I don't want to end up relying on them."

"You won't Jodie, the doctor will be able to lower the dosage in a controlled way so that you don't become addicted. You need them to help you sleep after everything that's happened."

"I told Jodie what we talked about at work the other day. Honestly, your secret is safe with me, I won't tell a soul." Mark smiled.

"Uh, I hope you don't mind Jodie, I was just so worried about you I had to get it off my chest."

Jodie walked over to the kitchen door and wrapped her arms around him, kissing him gently on the mouth. "Honestly babe, it's ok. It's good to talk about things when you're worried instead of bottling it all up."

Mark turned away from the couple's moment of affection, inwardly smiling at his own presence.

All three made their way to the living room and Patrick sat down next to the balcony doors.

"So, what have you two been doing with yourselves then?" Mark asked.

"Well, actually I have something to tell Jodie," Patrick said.

"What?" Jodie asked curiously.

Patrick smiled, "What would you say to a country break?"

"What do you mean?"

"You remember Auntie Beth, my mums Auntie?"

Jodie smiled nervously, not knowing what was coming next, "Yes, what about her?"

"Well, you know she left the cottage to my mum in her will? What would you say to a trip down to Loch Lomond for a week?"

Jodie's smile widened and she looked at Mark. "Did you know about this?"

"Me? Not at all, it sounds good though," Mark smiled at Jodie.

"Are you being serious? What about the case?"

Patrick moved to be beside Jodie, he held her hand and looked in to her tired eyes, seeing how exhausted she was, all the while being oblivious to the fact that the reason for this was sitting in the room with them.

"I've sorted it with Preston and Lang. I've told them that I'm taking you away for the week. You need to rest, I need to rest and recharge myself. We need some time together, just the two of us. Just think how nice it is there at this time of year, we can sit out on the decking watching the sun rise above the hills. We can relax in the fresh Scottish air and not have to worry about anyone else but ourselves, for a week anyway."

Jodie was quiet for a few moments as she regarded this. It did sound amazing, peaceful and almost tranquil. *Will I be able to shut out everything though, just because I'm not in Glasgow?* She asked herself.

Her thoughts were interrupted by Mark's voice. "If that doesn't sell it to you then I don't know what will."

Patrick laughed at this, all the while never taking his eyes off of Jodie. All he could think about was how much he wanted to take her away, make her happy again and take away her worry and stress.

Their relationship had lost out to the case in the last few weeks. They hadn't had a normal conversation, hadn't sat down to a meal together and they hadn't been intimate with each other in weeks. Patrick just wanted to get them back on track as they were so in love with each other and always had been. An outsider's perspective looking in at the relationship wouldn't have known this in recent weeks due to the circumstances.

"Well?" Patrick anticipated.

"Ok, let's go," she smiled.

As Patrick hugged Jodie, Mark stood up and went into the kitchen again. He thought about them going away for the week and how it would affect his plan. Just then, Patrick came in behind him. "Sorry mate, you must be feeling like a spare part just now."

Mark laughed. "No, I'm in the way here. I'll get going," he picked up his coat from the bar stool in the kitchen.

"Thanks," Patrick said.

"No worries, I know when I'm getting in the way of you know what." Mark gave a cheeky smile.

"No, I mean for listening to me the other night and not judging me, or Jodie for that matter."

"Hey, what are friends for?" Mark patted him on the shoulder.

As Patrick saw Mark to the door, Patrick picked up a leaflet for private hire cottages and lodges in the country.

"I meant to show you this. It's a leaflet for the cottage, just thought you would like to see it." Patrick handed Mark the leaflet.

"I thought you said your Auntie Beth used to own it and now it belongs to your mum?"

"Yeah she did own it before she and my dad died, then it was left to me. But it is in Lomond Park with other cottages and lodges and I rent it out through the year, but it is free for the next two weeks."

"Well, looks like you'll both have a great time. So, I'll see you in a week then?" Mark said.

"Looks like it. Enjoy work, hope it's not too mad while I'm away," Patrick smiled.

"Oh I'm sure I'll manage without you. The ladies will keep me busy I'm sure," Mark smiled a cheeky smile, the meaning behind it only known to him.

As Mark walked down the stairs of the landing, he looked at the leaflet Patrick had given him. He hadn't meant to leave the flat with it still in his hand, he had genuinely forgotten to hand it back. Patrick probably hadn't even given it a second thought. Mark made his way across South Street and walked through the underpass of the expressway.

As he walked silently, a thought entered his mind, a thought that would conclude Ross' plan and hopefully, end the grief that was wearing away his very soul.

As he walked along the busy street towards his own flat, Mark pulled out a letter from his back pocket. It was the letter from 'Adoption Contact Scotland,' the one that had been delivered the day that Billy Turner had been killed falling down those stairs. He sat down on a chair outside of a cafe and read the letter for the hundredth time.

Dear Mr Turner,

I write to you with regard to your application of contact with Jeffrey Turner. I am happy to tell you that Mr Turner has responded to our letter and has agreed to meet you in one of our centres.

It has to be said that your biological brother no longer goes by the legal name of Jeffrey Turner as his adoptive parents changed it when they took him into their care. Jeffrey now goes by the name of Patrick McLaughlin.

We cannot disclose any other personal information of Mr McLaughlin however there are no limits to which you can find out once you have met in our centre. Any information which you wish to disclose on the meeting is entirely at your own discretion. We have reserved an appointment for you both for October 25th 2010 in our centre in West Regent Street at 1pm. If we could have confirmation from you that this date is appropriate then you will be happy to hear that you will be meeting Patrick on this date.

If you have any questions please do not hesitate to call or pop in to the office.

Yours sincerely

M. Cairns (adoption contact director)

Mark smiled as he finished reading and calmly folded the letter and placed it back in the envelope. He got up and continued walking back toward Ross' flat.

Thirty Two

A relaxing journey

Jodie waited in the living room the next morning. She had packed her case and repacked Patrick's, just for something to do while she waited for him to come back from the car hire office just at the other end of South Street. As she sat on the couch she looked out of the glass doors.

The sky was a soft light blue and the sun shone so strongly that around it the sky almost looked white.

A perfect start to the break, she thought to herself.

She slid the door open and stepped out onto the balcony, feeling the heat from the early morning sun hit her face. It felt good on her skin. She closed her eyes and held onto the banister, allowing herself to relax a little more with each second she was blind to the view in front. The heat seemed to get stronger as she remembered the dream, the smoke and the overwhelming sensation of burning skin. She felt her throat tighten at the memory and opened her eyes instantly.

"I'm not allowing this to happen this week," she said aloud, almost as if she were convincing herself.

Jodie took a deep breath and was about to sit down on the chair behind her when she heard a car horn. She looked down to the entrance of the building and saw Patrick in the driver's seat of a red Nissan Micra.

"You ready yet?" he called up to her.

"Yep, I'll be right down."

Jodie went back inside and slid the door closed behind her. She turned the key in the door and closed the curtain half way and as she turned to leave the room she glanced in the mirror and saw Angela, Michelle and Rebecca all staring back at her, desperation in their faces. Jodie stopped to look back at them. She tried to stay calm and read any messages they were trying to get across, but they just stood there, staring at her. Pale faces, straggly hair and ragged clothes.

"What is it you want from me?" she said, desperation now in her own voice.

"Him," Michelle spoke now, her voice rough.

"Who? I don't know who you mean!" Jodie was shouting now.

But the girls were gone. All that stared back from the mirror now was her own reflection, her own tired eyes.

She heard the key turn in the front door and Patrick stood in the hall. "I realised you would need help with the cases. You ok?"

Jodie took a deep breath and tried her hardest to push everything to the back of her mind, just for now. "Yeah, I'm fine. Let's get out of here and have some fun."

***

The car journey was peaceful. They drove with the windows down and the stereo on mute. Jodie drank in the scenery all the way to the cottage. They passed several farms, stand alone houses and passed through a few villages on the way to Lomond Park. There was not a single cloud in the sky and the breeze which filtered through the windows was warm.

"Already I am feeling relaxed," she said.

"Good, I am glad that you are looking forward to this. It is exactly what we both need," Patrick replied.

They were cruising down the boulevard at a comfortable seventy miles per hour when Jodie closed her eyes and sunk into the seat. As she felt the breeze on her face and in her hair, she felt herself drift in and out of sleep. This was the first time in weeks that she had closed her eyes and not saw anything in her head which *she* had not put there. All she saw now was Patrick. She couldn't remember the last time that she and Patrick had been together in any way you can be, with someone you're in love with.

When they first became intimate, it was the first time for her at all and she knew that it would only ever be him. Anytime that they were apart, it felt like the other had taken a part of them away, like a part of them was missing and when they were together again, the puzzle piece would click back in to its original place. In the last few weeks, Jodie had forgotten how happy she could be, how much he made her feel safe and how much she wanted to be wrapped up in him. She wished she could feel like this forever, but she knew that in a week, this feeling would be gone again and she would lose a part of herself once more.

"All I want is for this to be over, to figure it out and just get back to us," she thought to herself as she drifted off.

She had said this aloud as she fell asleep, not aware of it. Patrick felt his stomach flip, knowing now that she felt the way he did. He wanted it over as soon as it could be. He was sick of this guy being invisible to his mind. Why couldn't they just show him who killed them?

What the hell is it that's stopping you from showing me his face? Patrick gritted his teeth at the thought of his own blindness.

He went over it in his head a thousand times, the black silhouette, the injuries, the faces he saw every minute of the day and night, the messages that had supposed meaning but to him meant nothing. He decided not to wrack his brain any longer.

This is where my minds rest begins, he thought to himself.

"You really think that you can't put this out of your mind for one whole week?"

Patrick looked over at Jodie, who was still sitting back, feeling hugged by the seat.

"Hey you, my thoughts are supposed to be private you know," he smiled gently.

"Sorry, I couldn't help it," she smiled back.

It was one thing that they barely did, to listen to each others thoughts. It was a rarity for psychics but for them, it was almost like they were one person, which can most definitely hinder a relationship. They had agreed not to listen to each others thoughts, but for some reason they were both fine with it at the moment. They both knew that this gift would help them to reconnect. Patrick took his hand from the gear stick and placed it over hers, squeezing it gently.

"I have a few things to tell you, a few things that I think may be the cause of my sleepless state," Jodie said.

"Ok, but not now. Let's just relax and enjoy the rest of the journey. We rarely get out of the city, I want us both to enjoy the calmness and tranquillity of the country."

That was fine by Jodie, for now it was *just* them, no deaths, no spirits and no worries, just the two of them. The way it had always been up until now. Nobody had ever fully understood their relationship or them as individuals. That was the way they liked it. That was the way that they had always wanted it to be. Their love for each other was one of a kind, unique and it felt like it had been slipping away. Jodie had felt like it was out with her control, but she wanted to get it back and so did Patrick.

He lifted her hand and kissed it gently, all the while keeping his eyes on the road.

"I won't let this break us Jodie, I promise. You will get better because I am going to figure this out. They've asked me to help and I will," he kept her hand firmly in his as he spoke. Jodie smiled, she loved his passion for the case, but she loved him more. She felt guilty that she wanted him to stop, but stopping wasn't an answer. If he stopped it wouldn't go away, it would just follow them everywhere, haunt them.

"I know Patrick," she said. But she didn't know. She could only hope with all her heart.

Thirty Three

Intervention

As they arrived at the cottage Jodie looked around her. There were cottages and lodges darted all around the place, but not too close to one another that people would be able to see inside but not too far away that they couldn't say hello to their neighbours that would be living by them for the week. But that would be *all* Jodie would say in passing, she just wanted peace for her and Patrick this week.

The cottage was beautiful and it looked onto the loch and over the hills. The scenery was stunning, the hills were emerald green and the loch mirrored the sky. There were now a few clouds darted across the sky, small but fluffy, almost like looking at cotton wool hovering above them. The grass around their feet had been cut to within an inch of its life, like a golf course patch of grass and its colour was like lime, not a blade out of place. The whole place looked like an artists painting.

"You like?" Patrick asked as he unloaded the bags from the boot of the Micra.

Jodie turned to him and smiled. "Who wouldn't? This place is amazing. Makes you really appreciate Scotland for what it is," Jodie replied as she gazed at her surroundings.

"It sure does," he said as he placed the bags at the front door of the cottage.

She walked over to the door to help Patrick inside with their belongings. The front door was blue, the same colour as the sky and there was a holly bush next to it. Again the leaves were brilliantly green and the berries were blood red. "Everything is so colourful here," she said as Patrick put the key into the lock.

"I know it's gorgeous," he replied as he opened the door.

He went inside and Jodie peered into the cottage. It was all open plan, like something from a winter fairy tale. There was a large brick fireplace in the centre of the back wall, with a pile of wooded logs next to it. On top there was a long row of large scented candles and above them, a large painting of the scene that she had just been looking at outside.

"Isn't that a painting of the view outside?" Jodie asked.

"Yep, Auntie Beth painted it herself," he said proudly.

"Seriously? It is absolutely stunning. I didn't know she was an artist."

"Not an established one anyway, she just painted for pleasure. She could have made some real money out of it if she had wanted to but that's not what she was all about," Patrick said as he unzipped the bags.

Jodie looked around once more and saw that in the far right of the cottage was a little living area with large cushiony sofas with fluffy blankets draped across the back and a stack of novels on a small side table, mostly murder mysteries and thrillers.

"Think I will be tackling some of those this week," she motioned to the stack.

"That's what they're there for, do you want to unpack then we can get some food?" Patrick asked.

"Yeah, sounds good, I'm starving."

Jodie took her bag into the small bedroom at the back of the cottage which was just off the kitchen. The room was white with dark wooden windows and little white netted curtains. The bed was almost as big as the room with drawers underneath to store belongings. For the cottage being so old fashioned, the bedroom was en-suite. The bathroom was quite big with a large white iron bath in the middle and a shower in the corner. The wall had a built in mirrored cabinet, twin sinks and a small plain glass window with another netted curtain over it.

"I love this," Jodie said to herself.

Patrick walked into the bathroom behind her. "It's cool isn't it?" he asked.

"Aw Patrick I love it, I can totally see us living here," she suddenly yawned.

"Do you want to go for a sleep?"

"No, I'm fine. I just feel a little worn out from the journey. I'll just unpack quickly and we can go and get some food."

Patrick kissed her on the forehead and returned to the bedroom. Jodie began putting her toiletries into the wall cabinet. She placed in her toothbrush, hairbrush, deodorant and toothpaste, soap and moisturiser. Then she placed in her bottle of sleeping tablets.

That looks a little out of place, she thought to herself. She sighed at the thought of being reduced to taking tablets to help her reach sleep, but then accepted that without them she was a complete insomniac. She closed the mirrored cabinet and looked at her reflection, much expecting to see a face or feel the burning of her skin, or hear the screams of the women's spirits. She held her breath, waiting for something to happen, but nothing did.

Good, I need to be normal, even if it is just for a week, her silent words meant for the spirits. Then a shadow quickly crossed the window of the bathroom. "Oh so you heard me then?" she said aloud.

"No, what did you say?" Patrick popped his head in to the bathroom.

"Oh, sorry, I was talking to myself," she smiled at him in the mirror.

"You ok?"

"Yeah I'm ok and I am ready to go. You ready?" she changed the subject.

They left the cottage and made the short trip in the car to the local shop to pick up their weeks supply of food.

***

The cottage door hadn't been locked and the lodges and cottages around were quiet, no one was around. The perfect opportunity was now and no other time would do. Ross quickly made his was into the cottage and headed straight for the bathroom, where he had watched Jodie unpack her things. He was aware that there wasn't a lot of time, so he made sure that he switched Jodie's pills as quickly as he could. He emptied the bottle and refilled it with a much stronger sleeping pill. Ross knew that by taking them, Jodie would be in such a deep sleep that she wouldn't have a clue what was going on around her. But then, he had another trick up his sleeve, just in case he needed it.

Ross finished his intervention and left the cottage, feeling very proud of himself. As he made his way back to the caravan site about two miles down the road he smiled and thought about how his plan had taken the turn that it did.

"If Patrick hadn't given me that leaflet for this place then this wouldn't have been possible. Thanks mate, I definitely owe you one," he said aloud through his callous grin.

As he drove to the caravan site, he saw Patrick and Jodie pass him on the road in the car that he had followed to Lomond Park. They did not look at him as they passed, there was no reason to. They did not know who he was, for the transformation from Mark to Ross was outstandingly different.

He kept his eyes on the road as he drove on, thinking of the outcome of his ways. Thinking of his mum, his dad and the way his life had taken the drastic turn. He thought about Patrick and Jodie and the way *their* lives would take a drastic turn, a deserving turn as he saw it.

He reached the caravan park and went inside to the small caravan that he had rented out for the week. He had placed all of his collection on the walls of his surroundings so that he wouldn't lose his inspiration for what he was doing. All he had to do was look at Maria's photograph and he would feel the pain once more trying to burst out of his chest and his head would throb.

He lit a cigarette from his pack and sat back on the chair in the small living area of the caravan. "Time to finish this once and for all," he said as he drew on the tip of the cigarette. As he blew the smoke out it entangled itself within the mist of the spirits who had been watching him. They tracked him as he followed Patrick and Jodie to Lomond Park, they needed every bit of information possible so that they could forewarn Patrick and Jodie of anything that was going to happen and try to make them see before it was too late.

They encircled him as did the smoke, listened to his thoughts and his plans for the couple. As they listened, Michelle's spirit became so angry that she began using her energy to try to frighten him. As he smoked the last of his cigarette, he reached over and took the photographs of the three girls down from his wall and he stared blankly at them. He said nothing, but his thoughts told the story of what happened to each of them. This made Michelle's anger grow uncontrollably and she used her energy to move any object she could find.

Ross heard a scraping sound, like a piece of cutlery being dragged across a kitchen worktop. He looked up and to his dismay saw exactly that, a fork being moved across the surface of the kitchen worktop.

"What the *fuck*?" he exclaimed as he stood up to get a clearer look. As soon as the words were out of his mouth he had to duck to avoid the fork connecting with his face. He turned when he heard it bounce off the window of the caravan and land on the floor.

Ross stared at the fork on the floor and couldn't believe what he had just witnessed. In his own mind, he was beginning to think that everything that had happened in his life was sending him insane. *I am losing it, I need to finish this before I really lose it,* he thought to himself as he lay in the small camp bed in the caravan.

He didn't sleep much for the rest of the night.

Thirty Four

Anna

Preston was sat at his desk filling out the endless amount of paperwork he had been putting off and Lang was sat at his own desk opposite Preston doing the exact same when the phone rang.

"Hello, D.S Preston speaking?"

Lang watched Preston's face as he sat there listening to what the caller was telling him.

"What is it?" he whispered.

Preston held his hand up to quieten Lang for a moment. Lang obeyed as the look on Preston's face was not a happy one.

"Damn! OK we'll be right there," he slammed the phone down.

"What?" Lang could have predicted what was about to be said.

"There's been another murder." Preston was already putting on his jacket.

"Shit!" Lang felt his stomach turn. "What do we know?"

"All I have been told is a young woman was found in the canal next to Kelvingrove Park about one hour ago!"

As they continued the conversation they were running to the car in the car park behind the station. All Preston wanted was to click his fingers and be at the scene. Preston started the car and Lang did not have time to put on his belt before they roared out of the car park.

"What are we going to do if it's the same guy?" Lang asked.

"What makes you think it's *not* the same guy?"

Lang took the point, so he was quiet for the remainder of the journey, which did not take long. They arrived at the side entrance to Kelvingrove Park and it had been blocked off by police tape. They showed their badges to the beat officers guarding the scene after fighting their way through the press and the flashing of cameras and bombardment of questions. A tent had been set up around the scene and Preston and Lang were able to gain access to the tent.

"You got here fast," the coroner said handing them both face masks and a pair of latex gloves.

"What's the story then?" Preston asked immediately as he put on the mask and gloves.

"Most likely strangulation, as you can see here and here," he pointed to the females neck. "The bruising is most likely to have been caused by finger grip."

Lang inspected the bruising as Preston continued to speak, "We're looking at a serial killer here aren't we." It wasn't a question.

"I'd say, most certainly," replied the coroner.

"Does this female have a name?" Preston asked.

"Yes, she has been identified by the driving license in her bag as Miss Anna Roper, twenty three years old," the coroner replied, shaking his head in disappointment.

"Thank you, could you send a report to the office? We'll need to inform the family," Preston said.

"It's on its way," the coroner replied. As they left the tent, Preston stood up on the hill slightly looking down on the newest crime scene.

"I'll phone Patrick, let him know," Lang said.

"Yeah, that's good." Preston felt devastated. He felt like he was failing the families of the already deceased and now another girl had wound up dead.

"This guy has got to be some kind of ninja for no one to notice anything," Lang said as he dialled Patrick's number.

"Yeah, tell me about it."

The phone rang on the other end a few times before Patrick answered. "Hello?"

"Patrick, it's Jim, I've got some bad news unfortunately."

"What is it?"

"Another woman has been found murdered in the canal at Kelvingrove Park, same injuries as the other girls," he said it with sadness in his voice.

There was a pause at the other end of the phone.

"Are you sure it is linked?" Patrick asked.

"Absolutely, it would be a major coincidence if it wasn't."

Patrick felt his heart skip a beat at the news. This was never going to end. "What was her name? I'll see if I can make a link with the other spirits," Patrick said.

"A Miss Anna Roper," Lang replied.

Patrick had a feeling of Déjà vu but it quickly passed. "Anna Roper... I know that name I think."

"You do? How is that?" Lang asked.

"I don't know, maybe it's just a common name. Anyway, thank you for letting me know."

Lang hung up and went to see if Preston was alright.

"In all my years of doing this Jim, I have never seen a serial killer. I don't know how we're going to solve this. This guy is a complete pro."

"Paul, he may be one step ahead now, but we'll catch up soon enough. He'll get what's coming to him. Just wait and see."

"I hope you're right Jim because if you're not I think that this case could end us," Preston said.

Lang knew it was possible but he didn't show it. "It won't come to that at all, we'll get him and we will put him away for a very long time, trust me."

"Like I said, I hope you're right. Come on, we need to get back to the station."

Telling a family that one of their own had been murdered was the worst part of the job for Preston and in this particular case he felt like he had done it one to many times. This killer was more than one step ahead of him and Lang, he was a million steps ahead. Preston really felt deep down in the pit of his stomach that this killer was unstoppable, and determined to keep going, striking when it was least expected. As they got into the car Preston sat in silence for a few moments. Lang allowed his partner time to cool down.

"You know what I see each time another young girl like Anna is found dead?" Preston said.

"A truck load of paperwork and a brick wall?" Lang suggested feeling just as pissed as Preston.

"My two girls, I see their faces. Because it could be them next you know."

"No way Paul, don't think like that." Lang put a comforting hand on his shoulder.

"Why not? Anything's possible here. They go out with their friends in Glasgow, they could fall prey to him just like the last four did."

"Well then, let's make sure no one else does, let's get back to the station and follow up on every damn lead we can, CCTV, witnesses, the lot. Come on, we're not going to get the bastard just sitting here are we?" Lang said.

Preston turned the key and made the journey back to the station.

Thirty Five

A new spirit

Patrick sat down on the sofa and put his head in his hands. How could this have happened again? Patrick felt extremely angry for Anna and for Angela, Michelle and Rebecca. He'd let them down, failed as a medium and now he felt like he had to start all over again.

Jodie walked out of the bedroom and saw Patrick sitting in the living area. "Patrick, what's wrong?"

"I just got off the phone with Lang," he took a deep breath. "There's been another murder."

Jodie sat back and absorbed what she had just been told and as the realisation sunk in she suddenly felt the tears fill her eyes. "Oh God, when did this happen?"

"This morning, she was found in the canal at the entrance to Kelvingrove Park, same injuries as the others too." Now he was holding Jodie, offering comfort.

"Oh no, that's awful. Was she of the same description as the others? What was her name?" Jodie was crying now, wishing that all of it would just go away.

"I haven't seen a picture of her yet, but her name was Anna Roper and she was twenty three apparently."

Jodie thought about the girl and wondered how long it would take before she began presenting herself and how with Anna being the fourth murder victim, it probably wouldn't take that long. As Jodie was lost in her thoughts she hadn't noticed Patrick leave the cottage to stand outside and let the new devastating information sink in.

As he watched the clouds floating slowly over his head he felt his stomach knot and pull at the thought of another victim to the sick person who got a buzz from strangulation. The anger began to build from the pit of Patrick's stomach and before he knew it he had punched the front door of the cottage. Jodie jumped out of her skin and ran to the door. When she opened it she almost laughed out of relief that it was only Patrick at the door and not another episode in her head.

"What are you doing?" she asked when she saw that Patrick's knuckles were bleeding.

"Punching the door, what does it look like?" he snapped.

Jodie was stunned at his outburst. "Alright no need to snap," she said as she took his hand in hers and led him in to the kitchen.

"I'm sorry, I'm just so *bloody* angry. I feel like I am failing this case and failing those girls."

"You are not failing the case Patrick, you will solve it, maybe not now but you will," she said as she dabbed at his knuckles with a tissue.

"But I have to solve it now, it's already too late. He's killed again and gotten away with it once more."

Patrick was so angry that for a moment Jodie thought that she was getting in his way and annoying him rather than helping him, "Do you want me to leave you alone?" she asked.

"What? Oh no, I'm sorry babe I didn't mean to make you feel uneasy. God, you've had enough to deal with without me making it worse." He took her face in his good hand and kissed her gently on the mouth. As he did so, she connected with his mind and as they kissed she listened quietly, so he wouldn't hear her in his thoughts.

His mind was sad and tangled in the frustration of the case and Jodie's own, tired mind. She could feel the pain he felt in his chest, not a physical pain but one of grief. He was grieving for the relationship that they once had. It was not the same as it once was, before the case took it away from them. He loved Jodie with every breath, every blood vessel, every blink. She could feel the weight of everything slowly pushing him down and she knew that in some way it would break him. She pushed her lips to his, harder now and for the rest of their moment, she pushed the thoughts from his head and filled it with happier times. She felt him relax as she did so and as they made love they both forgot about the murders, only for a short time, but it was enough to make Patrick realise later that enough was enough. No longer would this take up his life, he was sick of the stress and anxiety that they both felt.

They lay on the couch with a large tartan blanket over them and even though Jodie was silent he knew she was awake as her breathing was gentle and light.

"Marry me?" he asked.

"What do you mean? We're already engaged," she said bewildered by his question.

"I know that, but I mean let's *actually* get married. When all this is over, let's just do it. There's nothing to say we can't is there?"

Jodie looked into his eyes and regarded his words, "Are you being serious?"

He smiled. "Yes, I am. So?"

Jodie's smile widened and she immediately flung her arms around him. "Of course I want to get married, it's all I have ever wanted."

As they held each other in their arms, their happiness beamed all around the room. Jodie felt like she had the most energy she had ever had and Patrick felt like his whole body was smiling. But the thought never left the back of his mind, not really. The killer was still out there and it could take a long time before he was caught. The spirits never left his mind either and they never would, not until Ross Turner was caught, behind bars or dead, it had to be done.

Jodie fell asleep with a subtle smile on her face and Patrick held her for the rest of the night and as he fell asleep, his dreams were filled with nothing, whereas Jodie's were filled with the screams of Angela, Michelle and Rebecca and a new voice.

Anna Roper.

But she wasn't just screaming in terror at the prospect of her own murder. She was screaming at the prospect of another on the way.

Jodie awakened in a cold sweat and sat bolt upright, with the feeling of burning skin and suffocation. She was alone in the room.

No Patrick. No killer. Just alone.

Thirty Six

Injection of fear

She splashed her face with cold water, trying desperately to wash away the dream, the screams, the burning.

Why is this happening to me? She thought to herself.

The cottage was dark and silent, she looked into the bedroom from the bathroom and the digital clock read 2:10 a.m, another sleepless night ahead of her then.

She splashed her face once more and dabbed it with the towel as she stood quietly over the sink. She replayed the dream over and over again in her head, wondering why yet again she had the burning sensation slowly creeping over her skin and now the feeling of suffocation. A new face now haunted Jodie's thoughts, Anna Roper. As if things weren't stressful enough, now she had to cope with a new spirit.

She opened the mirrored wall cabinet and took out her bottle of sleeping pills. She swallowed one with a glass of water and closed her eyes, not being able to bare the sight of her own reflection, I look so tired and unwell, she thought.

She was startled as she suddenly felt Patrick wrap his arms around her waist. "Are you ok?" he whispered.

"Yeah, bad dream."

"Tell me," he kissed her neck.

"No, honestly it's nothing."

"Now, I don't believe that for a minute," he kissed her neck again.

She sighed knowing that he didn't believe her. "Well, if you really want to know, I had a dream about Anna Roper."

Patrick stopped kissing her neck and spun her around to face him. "A dream or a vision?"

"A bit of both to be honest, it was awful Patrick. And I had that feeling again, the burning, like my skin was on fire."

He was hugging her before she had finished speaking, almost squeezing her. His face showed courage and confidence that things would be ok but his mind spoke a thousand words of fear and worry for his fiancée. "Jodie it was just a dream, you wouldn't have had it if we hadn't found out about Anna."

Jodie considered this but immediately dismissed it. "No. I'm beginning to think that they are trying to tell me something."

"Like what?" he asked calmly to keep her from becoming upset.

"I don't know. But I think they are trying to tell me that something is going to happen but I can't see what it is," her voice began to wobble.

Patrick held her tightly as she began to cry and through her tears he could see the fear of the unknown in her eyes, "It's going to be ok. I promise I won't let anything happen to you, or me for that matter."

"I don't think it's that simple Patrick."

"Trust me, it is," he said as he wiped away her tears.

He led Jodie back in to the bedroom and tucked her in to the bed linen like a mother would with their young child. He climbed in beside her and wrapped her in his arms. "Just sleep baby, I'm here and I will keep you safe."

Jodie quickly drifted off unexpectedly and before Patrick knew, Jodie was breathing slow and steady.

She was in a deep sleep now.
***

The car was packed and ready to go. The black double sided tape and rope lay in the boot of the car and he made sure that the one most important thing he needed was easily accessible. He had dressed himself in black from head to toe and he ensured that the only part of his face that could be seen were his eyes, not even the skin around his eyes or eyebrows, just the eyes themselves! He rubbed his hands together as he observed the equipment that he had required for his plan, the plan that had only come together in the last two days. The car hire company were the only people who knew that he had the car and by the time everyone else knew about him it would all be over anyway.

"Not long to go now Mum, I will be seeing you very soon," he said as he sat in the car looking at her photograph.

He got out of the car and leaned against it. He looked up at the sky and all he could see were the twinkling of the stars and the blackness that was the night, well early morning, 2:30 a.m to be precise. Being in Loch Lomond made Ross appreciate his surroundings a little more than usual, there was no light polluting the night sky, blocking the stars from the human eye. The moon shone almost like a light bulb without a shade. It lit up the tops of the hills and lit up the Loch. The water was still and nearby came the trickling sound of a small stream.

The chill in the air was pleasant on his skin and it made Ross relax. "I'm going to enjoy this," he said as he observed his surroundings.

Ross Turner turned his back on the beautiful scene to get into the car and felt frozen to the spot in which he stood. He wanted to move, but a fear washed over him, a fear that he couldn't identify. Ross slowly felt his fingers become numb, his feet felt as if they were sinking in to the ground and the more he tried to move the more fearful he became. Unaware, the spirits swirled around him, slowly, haunting his every move, every thought, every idea.

He tried to move and as he did, the energies of now all four spirits crushed his physical movement. Michelle became angrier each time an attempt was made to reach for the car door or to move a step closer. Her energy pushed down on him, making his head feel heavy. His chest began to feel tight, breathing quickened. His head felt like it was about to pop and if he could have seen his face he was positive it would be a vibrant red colour. Ross tried desperately not to panic, but seeing as he assumed he was having a panic attack he found it some what difficult. He slowed his breathing, attempting deep, long breaths. As he began to calm, Rebecca moved in, allowing her energy to wrap him up. A new wave of panic set in and now his heart was beating so hard and fast that he felt it could burst out of his chest. Angela pulled Rebecca back, for now. Their energies must be used for a more appropriate time.

Ross Turner climbed in and quickly started the car and shot off down the road, the engine becoming a dull roar the further away it became.

They allowed him to breathe again. But Anna did not leave him, she stayed by him, watched his every move. She would not rest until she saw him suffer. Her spiritual purpose was to see Ross Turner die and even if it took a hundred years, Anna was prepared to be stuck in between planes until that day would come.

Thirty Seven

Kidnap

Lomond Park was in complete darkness when he had arrived. Every lodge and cottage had no sign of life, all lights were out and no one was around. He had entered the park quietly, leaving the car behind a large bramble bush at the entrance. He hadn't wanted to take the car in, he couldn't risk stirring up an unsuspecting audience. As he walked along the path he could see the cottage in the distance.

He held onto the small bottle in his pocket and was already wearing the small face mask under his balaclava. His gloves were thermal but bore a leather exterior.

As he watched the cottage grow in his vision he began to feel the throbbing in his head and the pain in his chest.

Soon, he thought to himself as he picked up his pace. All he could think of was bursting into the cottage and creating a bloody mess, *a massacre*. The anger was becoming unbearable but he managed to contain it as he made his way, closer now to the cottage.

"The pills should have worked by now, if she has taken them that is," he said under his breath.

He reached the cottage, still careful not to attract anyone to his presence. He made his way towards the bedroom window, aware that his footsteps sounded louder than usual in the quiet of the night. He peered through and to his expectations both Patrick and Jodie were asleep. He then made his way around to the front of the cottage and tried the door handle.

It opened.

Ross couldn't help but to think that this was all just a little too easy and that something was going to stop him before he could finalise his plans.

Easy does it, he thought to himself as he pushed the door open. Careful of his tread, watching out for obstacles in his path he made his way to the bedroom. The cottage was so dark, darker than dark itself and something felt odd to him. He stopped and turned to scan the room but saw nothing. But he could feel...

Suddenly, a vase flew at him, full speed towards his face. His instinct was to duck, but instead he caught the vase.

You're not getting rid of me that easily. He wasn't sure who his thought was directed at but he was pissed that his plan was becoming more difficult than he had anticipated.

Ross realised that he did not feel frightened by a vase being thrown in his direction by someone who wasn't really there, but more angry that the vase could have halted his plan immediately.

If the air in the cottage could have growled, it would have. The anger between the spiritual energies was like electricity, willing themselves to pass through him like ten thousand volts and stop him dead! But his own will was too strong for them, even though they put all of their energies together.

He placed the vase quietly on the couch as he passed it and continued on his path. As he entered the bedroom where the mediums slept, he understood what he had felt moments ago at the car.

They're protecting her, he thought to himself as he creepily approached the bed, blending in with the darkness.

He's going to be the tricky one, Ross thought to himself as he reached into his pocket. He brought out a muslin cloth and from the other pocket he brought out a brown coloured glass bottle which looked like a cough syrup bottle. He soaked the muslin cloth in the liquid inside the bottle.

Chloroform.

He placed it very carefully over Patrick's nose and mouth, but did not apply pressure. He wanted to smash the cloth into Patrick's face however he knew that doing it was not in his own best interests. Ross waited until Patrick's breathing became irregular before he made his move.

As he listened, Patrick's breathing had become raspy. Ross had given him enough to keep him unconscious while he carried out his plan, but not too much that it would kill him, perhaps leave him with life long breathing problems yes, but not enough to kill him.

No, no Patrick, I want you to see this as much as I want to enjoy it, Ross couldn't help smiling as he watched Patrick lying there. He made his way around the bed now, towards his goal.

Jodie was completely and utterly dead to the world. *I see my little prescription worked then,* he thought to himself as he smiled under his balaclava. He thought back to when he had switched the pills. It had been so easy it was as if Jodie *wanted* him to do it.

He took out another muslin cloth and again soaked it in the Chloroform, now placing it over Jodie's nose and mouth. Again he fought off the urge to smash the cloth into her face, as much as he wanted too, it wasn't part of the plan, it could ruin everything. And killing them both here while they slept was far too easy. The satisfaction that Ross needed to stay well would need to come from a situation where challenge was the biggest obstacle.

Jodie's breathing also became raspy and that's when he made his move, he didn't have long. He quickly lifted the cloth from Patricks face and then he used all of his strength to throw Jodie over his shoulder and carry her out of the cottage, not before dropping a note on the dining table in the kitchen, "Something for your man to read over breakfast," he smirked as he left the cottage.

He ran to the car and when he got there he opened the boot with his free hand and almost threw Jodie inside. She was still out cold, but he knew it wouldn't be long before she came too and he needed to be sure that they were on the road before then.

He taped her ankles and wrists together and taped over her mouth. "This has all been too easy Jodie, just a shame for you the car journey won't be so easy," he whispered in her ear. Ross took one last look at her before he slammed the boot closed.

Thirty Eight

The beginning of revenge

The continuous bumping sensation was what finally woke her up. It only took one second to realise that her eyes were open but she could see absolutely nothing. Then after two seconds she realised that her hands and ankles were taped together (taped and not tied for the movement of her hands and ankles made her skin feel like it was beginning to tear) and after the third second of consciousness was when she tried to call out, making her realise that her mouth was also taped closed!

What the hell is going on? She thought. There came another bump, harder now. She wriggled, tried to throw her body around to escape from where she was.

I'm in a car, she spoke in her mind. *Who the hell is driving?*

She was awake for what seemed like a long time, feeling every crack and bump on whatever road to which she travelled on. There was no music, no conversation to be heard or voice to be recognised.

She panicked silently, not knowing who was driving the car, where the car was going... was she going to die?

She asked herself this over and over, tears falling across the bridge of her nose and onto the oil scented floor of the boot which she lay in. Her left side ached, feeling bruised as she was thrown around the small space she had been forced to lie in. The longer she lay in the boot, the more she began telling herself she was going to die, almost preparing herself. Then she remembered the conversation she had had with Patrick, when was it? She had no idea how long she had been gone, or if Patrick even knew she was away. Would he be looking for her? She had dreamt of the girls again, felt the burning of her own skin, the wind pipe in her neck being choked. She had wondered if the spirits were trying to warn her of something that was still to come.

Oh my god, I'm in the killer's car! She screamed in her head.

The car came to a stop. She felt the engine die, her ears were ringing. The door to the car slammed, footsteps now approaching. Her heart was now slamming against her chest, her throat as dry as sand and her eyes streamed. Then came the screaming, the words, the name *Mark, Ross, Mark, Ross, Mark, Ross*.

It was all she could hear now, no more ringing, no more footsteps, the words in her head spoken by an amalgamation of voices, those voices crying in terror. The fear that had taken over her body made her tremble and shake as she heard the handle of the boot click open.

***

The sun shone over the hills and through the crack in the curtains of the kitchen. Patrick was sitting at the dining table holding the note in his hand;

If you're as psychic as you say you are then you will know damn sure where to find her won't you Patrick. Why don't you ask your little spirit friends to help join in the chase.

As Patrick dialled Preston's number he held onto the note, his eyes stinging due to the fact that he had been drugged and also, he hadn't blinked since reading the note.

"Patrick, to what do I owe this fine pleasure?" Preston answered chirpily.

"It's Jodie. She's gone."

"What?"

"Gone, kidnapped, stolen, whatever you guys call it!"

"You sure she's not just gone for a stroll down at the Loch or something?" Preston hoped that the thought hadn't crossed Patrick's mind yet and saying this would calm him down. The silence after the question made him realise it already had.

"There's a note." Patrick felt his anger raise him from his seat, "It's from him."

Preston didn't know what to make of this, he kept his eyes on Lang the whole way through their conversation giving him the knowledge that they had a severe problem on their hands. "What does it say?" Preston asked.

Patrick read the note to him slowly through gritted teeth, "and the bastard drugged us."

"What?" more disbelief in Preston's voice.

"I found two muslin cloths on the floor of our bedroom when I woke up and they were both damp. One was obviously mine to keep me out of the *fucking* way!" Patrick had to stop grinding his teeth or they were about to shatter under the pressure.

"What do they smell like?" Preston asked.

"I don't know. It's a sweet smell whatever it is."

Preston had an idea of substance that was on the cloth. "How's your head?"

"Sore and my vision is a little blurry, why?"

"I think I know what he has used to drug you. We need to test them to be sure though."

Patrick didn't know what to do, he was feeling every emotion under the sun and as it began to boil to the surface he felt his patience slipping. "Preston, what do we do now?"

"Right, we're on our way," Preston said as he tried to put his jacket on with his free hand.

"No! What's the point in that?"

"To start searching for Jodie of course!"

"No, I'm coming to you. If the killer is going to repeat history, then he is going to do it in Glasgow. And the closer I get to Glasgow then there's more of a chance I will be able to pick up on Jodie's presence and we will find her." Patrick had already locked up the cottage and was now in the car.

"But you've been drugged, you can't drive Patrick, it's not safe."

"Are you going to stop me? My fiancée is in danger of being murdered and you want me to stay put because I have a slight headache. Not a chance, arrest me if you have too!"

Preston hesitated for just a moment, "Ok, meet us at the station and we'll take it from there," he was still trying to put his jacket on, he didn't know why.

"I will be there in the next thirty minutes, oh and I have the cloths too." Patrick said.

The whole time Patrick was in the car, he pictured the note in his head over and over and he continued to repeat what he had said about being able to pick up on Jodie's presence the closer he got.

But where are they? he asked himself.

And even though he refused to say it into himself or out loud, he knew that if he didn't pick up on her presence, it would mostly likely mean she was unconscious.

Or dead.

***

He raised the boot slowly, holding it open. She looked up at him, searching for a clue as to who had taken her. She did not recognise the eyes. She tried to speak through the tape but nothing came. The fear had muted her voice.

"Hello Jodie, comfortable are we?" he smiled at her. Her eyes stared in to his and he knew that she tried to recognise them. He felt a strange pleasure from this rush through his body, giving him a surge of adrenalin.

"Now, this won't hurt you, we just need to make sure that the next part of the adventure is as intriguing for you as the first part has been," as he spoke, he soaked another small muslin cloth in the Chloroform and this time he held it over her nostrils and applied pressure. There was absolutely nothing that she could do except for breathe in the chemical.

Her instinct was to fight, but with her hands and feet restricted, the overwhelming terror began to set in.

This must have been why I had the feeling of suffocation, she thought as she jerked with all her might as he closed in on her.

As she watched the cloth draw nearer to her face, she began to smell the sweet scent that came from it. It was surprisingly pleasant, but she knew that this was not a good thing.

Her head began to ache and her eyes began to sting as suddenly they were heavy in her head. She struggled as she tried to focus on his eyes, her own vision becoming blurry and weak. She couldn't fight it anymore, the sleep was coming and it was coming fast...

He had to fight the urge to suffocate her there and then, to will his hand to release the pressure that he applied to her nose. He stopped, pulled away. She lay there, motionless, breathing now clean air. He threw the soaked cloth into the boot alongside her and slammed the boot closed again. As he made his way to the driver's seat, he felt haunted by the sound of his own footsteps on the gravel. He stopped and turned slowly to look around him but saw nothing.

Although, the feeling of a presence all around him was strong. *Maybe it's just the presence of her that I can feel,* he thought to himself, trying to reassure his doubts.

He composed himself and opened the car door, again only to be stopped in his tracks by the feeling of company. Again, he turned. Nothing.

Then the sound of a raspy scream in his right ear! A cold hand on his neck.

But still, no one around.

He jumped in to the driver seat and locked the doors. "Get a grip Ross, you don't have a lot of time to get her there."

The rear wheels spun up the gravel as he sped off down the deserted road.

Thirty Nine

Setting the scene

Nothing meant more to him than his mother. Nothing on the earth could replace his mother. That is why it had all boiled down to this, the final chapter in his revenge, the last sacrifice. He wasn't scared, not at all. He wanted to go, to be able to have that chance to see his mother again. Patrick had said himself that spirits were contactable through him, so surely he had a chance of seeing her, especially if he was dead!

It had taken a lot of effort and time to get Jodie to where they were now without anyone seeing them. But the hard part was over and all he had to do now was wait for Jodie to wake up and the fun could begin.

He had laid her on the floor of the room, blacked out the window and made sure that she was in a position that she would see all of the pictures, photo's and cut outs...all of them.

The room was cold and a little damp, a perfect setting to wake up and realise you are still in the nightmare.

He left her in the room, still and asleep, a chemical induced sleep. She lay on the floor and as she did, her mind slipped into the dream stage of sleep, meaning that it would be soon that she would awaken, most likely feeling groggy from the chemical.

Ross hammered nails through wooden slats that he had placed across the frame of the door. The nails were long and thick and there was no way possible that she was able to open the door from the inside. He hammered in the last nail and sat down, head against the wall and waited for her to wake up.

***

She put every single shred of energy into making her legs move quicker than they were already but it was no use. She ran on the spot and in slow motion too, like what happens to people in most dreams they have that involve running.

They looked back at her as she tried with all of her might, and were screaming, "Come now, run with us, you have to tell Patrick!"

She could feel the sweat from her brow stinging her eyelids as she tried frantically to keep up with them. "Tell Patrick what?" she called back.

"It's him," they were crying, screaming, choking on their words.

"Who's him? I don't understand?" she was calling out over the shortness of breath.

She remembered the eyes staring into hers in the car, looking for a clue in the eyes but finding nothing. The voice played over in her head, the neurons firing through her brain, trying to make the connection. And that's when it clicked.

Him...

"Oh my god, it's Mark," she said quietly, but they still heard her.

Now they were smiling, yet still running. However, Jodie was standing still and not able to shift the heaviness from her legs. She watched them go out of sight, dreading the thought that she needed them now and they wouldn't be there.

She stopped her attempts to move from where she was and looked around. There was nothing, everything was gone. There was no road or ground, there were no trees, no cars, no people or sound.

"Where am I?" she said. She heard no reply to her open question, she felt lost. "Am I dead?" The next thing she knew, she was lying down on the blackness beneath her, rolled up in a ball and feeling very cold. She could hear a faint banging sound above her, but again she could see nothing.

Then the banging became louder and had more rhythm, BANG, BANG, BANG.

The pain in her head began to throb and memories began creeping their way back into her mind. She forced her eyes open and had to blink a few times as the blurriness was thick.

She instantly remembered the room from her dream and tried to lift her head from the cold floor. The pain resembled that of a tension headache and she tried to ignore it.

As she sat up, her hip also began to throb but she pushed it to the back of her mind when she saw the extent of her situation. The banging was coming loud and in a steady beat from the door of the room. She managed to stand and she walked over to the door and as she did she could feel the banging vibrate in her chest.

A new terror sped through her when she saw the photographs on the wall, Angela, Michelle, Rebecca and Anna smiled out at her. However this is not what created the feeling of despair and desperation in her veins.

Staring back at her was herself. A photograph taken from the small article about the church was neatly pinned next to his victims' faces. She could feel the tears stinging her eyes as she thought about Patrick. Did he even know she was gone, how long had it been?

BANG, BANG, BANG.

She jumped when the banging started again.

"Please let me go," she called out, attempting a brave firmness and failing miserably.

"Oh, you're up."

She held her breath when she heard the voice, shocked at the familiarity.

"So, are you comfortable in your new space, you're going to be spending a lot of time in there. Well actually that's a lie, you won't be spending too much time in there to be honest, ha."

Mark! She was too stunned to speak. She listened to him as he laughed on the other side of the door, the banging continued. She knew he was hammering nails into the wood.

She had already experienced this place in her dream...

Not dream, premonition, she heard in her head.

Then another realisation kicked in. The dreams, the panic attacks, lack of sleep, it was all linked to this moment.

"So, what do you think?" he asked calmly.

"Of what?" she replied, suddenly feeling equally calm.

"Your new room, I hope you like it," he laughed again.

Jodie slowly began pacing the room. "Why don't you quit the game and just kill me if that's what you plan on doing?"

"Oh Jodie, trust me darling, this is no game." His voice turned sinister as he spoke and she decided that it was time to face up to the harrowing truth that she was going to die in this room.

"Mark, I know it's you."

"Jodie, you don't know anything at all."

"Then tell me, tell me why you murdered four women for no reason?" she began to feel angry, all the while the tension headache beginning to travel down her spine.

Ross sat down outside the door to the room in his flat and brought his knees up to his chest. "Ah, so you heard about Anna then?"

"Of course we did. Patrick is working with police, remember?" Jodie was glad that she was on the opposite side of the door as she knew this would anger him.

"*Fucking* police, what's the point in that set up, it has been nine weeks, four murders already and they are still none the wiser." She heard the grin as he spoke.

"I wouldn't say they're none the wiser!"

"Oh yeah, why's that then? You going to use your psychic powers to talk to your precious little Patrick?" he taunted.

Jodie wished she could. But all she could do was hope that Patrick would figure out what was going on using his own abilities, although for the first time she highly doubted it.

She closed her eyes and hung her head, feeling sad and absolutely terrified, as well as angry.

"Jodie, what exactly do you think you know?"

"I thought I knew absolutely nothing?" she played him back at his game.

"Well, you're supposed to be the psychic, you tell me."

Jodie's eyes were still closed when she felt the presence around her. When she opened her eyes, she was stunned yet somehow relieved to see all four girls stood in front of her in the darkened room.

"Yes, I am psychic," she smiled slightly. The girls encircled her and she suddenly felt their energy become one and enter her own spirit.

"Well?" Ross was beginning to sound agitated. "Tell me!" he shouted loudly.

Jodie walked towards the door slowly, feeling tired. She pressed her face up against the door and said, "I'll tell you every intricate detail of what you did to me on the night you killed me." The voice was no longer raspy as it once was before, but clear and precise.

Ross stood up and backed away when he heard it. He didn't think he would remember a lot about the girls, as they didn't matter to him, but *that* voice sent chills up his spine. He knew exactly whose voice it was.

Michelle Levine.

Forty

Realisation

Jodie knew everything that was happening. She understood that what was happening was necessary and it was possible that it could save her. She allowed the girls to take over her mind but knew that at anytime she could take charge. She felt at ease with this.

"Tell me why Mark?" Jodie spoke.

Silence...

He won't speak now since Michelle scared the living day lights out of him, Angela said.

"Can't we have this conversation face to face?" Jodie asked, feeling her heart skip a beat at the suggestion.

Ross was still staring at the door from the other side in shock of hearing that voice.

How was it possible that he could hear that voice? Michelle was dead, killed by him.

"I can hear your thoughts you know," Jodie said.

"Aye, I'm sure you can," he struggled not to believe her.

"Yep, your wondering how you heard Michelle's voice." It wasn't a question.

Ross had never believed in spirits, ghosts and goblins and all that paranormal nonsense. However, now he wasn't so sure. "Actually, I am thinking that you put on a good act. You should be *shitting* yourself right now, but you're pulling off being brave. I kind of like it," he was trying to pull off being brave himself, the unknown forces within the room and the unexplained things that had happened to him scared him a little. But he would never show it. However, this feeling quickly passed as he thought of how his plan meant that he wouldn't have to deal with them for much longer.

"Look, I'm clearly not going to escape this, so I would at least like my last conversation with a human to be face to face," Jodie was terrified beyond belief, but she put her skills to good use.

When she was a child and first discovered that she was psychic, she didn't think that her ability had a name. Jodie thought that she was just mentally deranged. Who would believe that she could talk to dead people?

It scared her terribly when she was little but she learned how to be brave and how if she faced it head on, then it would go away and she wouldn't have to be scared of it. This was how she was dealing with the situation that had presented itself now. She was going to face it head on, although she knew that it wouldn't go away, *she* would be the one that would go away. She just hoped that it would be quick and painless.

"Are you seriously telling me that you want to be in the same room as me? A murderer?" He enjoyed the prospect.

She took a deep breath. "Yes, I want to see you. I want to talk to you face to face."

A few moments of silence on his part passed as he considered this. Jodie on the other hand was listening to all sorts of things in her head. It frustrated her a little as she was trying to listen to Mark's thoughts, which were quiet at this time.

***

An hour had passed silently. Jodie had heard nothing from Mark since she told him she wanted to see his face. She was beginning to think that he had decided to just leave her there, in the cold damp smelly room. But then a noise came that chilled her to the bone. She listened as Mark began pulling the nails out of the wood with what she thought to be pliers, what else would he use?

Her stomach lurched at the sound of each nail coming out of the wood, knowing that she was closer to seeing his murderous face. The girls in her head were barely making their presence known either but she knew they were still there.

Don't get too close to him, Anna's voice came now. *I made that mistake.*

Jodie nodded and backed herself against the window wall. The last nail was pulled from the wood and the last wooden slat dropped on the floor before she saw the handle turn as he opened the door. She held her breath as she watched the door open and in her head she heard a sound which resembled a growl which, she presumed was Michelle. This made her feel uneasy but she kept up the brave pretence.

Jodie was now face to face with a man that she did not recognise. "Hello Jodie."

Her face must have told a story of confusion because he then said, "Not who you were expecting?"

"Mark?" Jodie asked. She knew it was his voice, but the face was not his.

"Ross Turner. Mark is just my stage name," he said it like an announcer would introduce the next programme to come on the television.

The voices in her head were going crazy, all shouting and screaming at once. She couldn't pick out any particular sentences of who was saying what but she knew exactly what it all meant.

"That's why he couldn't figure it out sooner," Jodie said aloud before she could stop herself.

"What?" he asked.

She thought about it in her head before she said it out loud, *Multiple Personality Disorder. No, if he had that then he would be denying that he had killed them. He is just a sick evil man, using another identity to fool everyone.*

"You killed them as Ross but you became Mark to cover it up." She looked directly into his eyes as the realisation came to her. The fear tore through her, making her body tingle, making her sweat and she began to tremble as he slowly approached her.

Ross smiled harrowingly at her now. "Good girl Jodie. You should have been a detective."

The blow to the side of her face knocked her to the floor.

Forty One

Justification from a killer

Patrick pulled up outside the station and got out of the car. He stood and listened for a few moments, trying to hear something... anything.

But he heard nothing, only the early morning traffic. As he began to walk into the station, he saw a picture in his mind, a picture of the room Jodie was in. He couldn't see Jodie but he was being shown the wall with the photographs and reports that had been pinned on it.

It was like a slow motion home movie, taking him slowly from one side of the room to the other. It was at that moment that he saw the photograph of himself and Jodie, alongside information about the church. He could almost smell the dampness of the room. It was so dark and had such an evil feel to it. He knew then that this is where Jodie was, but he had no idea where this place was or how to get to it. He ran through the entrance of the station but didn't have to go very far to find Preston and Lang as they were in the reception area waiting for him.

"That was quick," Lang said.

"Roads were clear. Here..." he said handing Preston a plastic bag, "the cloths."

Preston handed the bag to Lang and Lang disappeared through a set of double doors behind him.

"So, what is the plan?" Patrick asked.

"Well, considering that we have absolutely nothing on the murderer, as much as I hate to say it then it is mostly up to you and what you can pick up," Preston replied.

"Ok, well I have been shown a room."

"A room?" Lang said as he came back through the doors.

"Yes, a room. I don't know where it is but I know that Jodie is there."

Lang could feel the frustration building inside him, almost as if it was using his intestines as a ladder, it slowly climbed but he managed to keep it under control.

"What does it look like?" Preston asked as he led Patrick and Lang back to their office.

"It's a horrible dark green colour, very dull and damp. I could smell the dampness."

Well that narrows it down, Lang thought to himself. Even after his experience at the church he still found Patrick hard to believe sometimes.

"There is one window but it has been blocked out, maybe by a wooden board or something. Then there is a wall and it is covered in photographs of Angela, Michelle and Rebecca. There are newspaper cuttings and reports from the murders. It's as if he has put them there to remind himself of who they were. He's one sick bastard!"

Preston was writing in his note pad as Patrick explained what he had seen.

"So you think that this is close?" Lang asked.

"Well, the guy must live locally. There is no way that he would come into Glasgow to kill someone then have to travel out of Glasgow to get home!" Patrick said.

"Yeah, that makes sense. So do you think you will be able to pick up where this place is?" Lang asked.

"Glasgow is a big place. It's impossible to think that we will find her," Patrick said.

Patrick knew that there was the highest chance that he wouldn't find Jodie. It wasn't the thought of her dying that ate away at him the most, it was the thought that she could die and he would never find her. Their mental communication cut off by her murder. The thought was slowly killing him.

***

She held her face as she looked up at him. Her cheek bone felt like it had exploded and was now burning under her flesh. He leered over her as she tried to regain her composure, she could smell his breath and his presence felt heavy over her.

"I am sorry, but your attitude was becoming a little too cocky for my liking!" he drew his eyes away from her and allowed her to sit up straight from lying on the floor.

"Why did you do it?" she asked.

He took a deep breath and walked over to the wall with the photographs on it. Jodie noticed that he had carelessly left the door open but she knew that now was not the time to run, he was too fired up and ready for her to make that move. No, she was going to bide her time.

"Don't even think about it!" he said, almost as if he knew what she had been thinking.

"Trust me, I am not going anywhere until you suffer." Michelle's voice came from Jodie's mouth and he spun around to face her.

"Stop doing that!" he shouted.

"It's not me, it's your victim." Jodie had no idea where her new found braveness had come from, maybe it was Michelle giving her the courage.

"It's bullshit is what it is, you're throwing your voice," he turned away from her again.

Jodie was getting annoyed with him but she knew she couldn't show it. If the spirits weren't careful and played around with him too much he may get too angry and that would leave Jodie in a difficult situation to say the least.

Stop winding him up, keep it cool for now, Jodie said into herself. She could see the other spirits agreeing with her but Michelle was not in a cooling off type of place at the moment and Jodie felt her energy lurch, throwing itself at him. Jodie heard her growl and for a moment Ross looked as though he had heard it too. She saw the hairs on his arms stand on end at that very moment she had heard the growl, but she acted as normally as she could in the given situation.

"You want to know why I killed those girls?" he asked.

"Not just me, they do too."

"Urgh, would you shut the *fuck* up about ghosts!" he shouted at her and he flew over to her and grabbed her by the upper arms. "You're a fucking human and when you die, that's it. None of this spirit haunting crap!" He was shaking her now.

Her head began to hurt as he shook her, but he soon stopped and just stared into her face. She stared back, looking for Mark. The only resemblance was the voice.

"*Whores!*" he said suddenly, causing Jodie to jump. His eyes widened like those of a madman.

"What?" she asked.

"That's why I killed them. They were whores, didn't deserve to live. Simple," he said it very matter of fact.

"I don't understand what you mean," she said.

"My mother killed herself, because of my poor excuse for a human *fucking* dad!"

Jodie couldn't keep up with him, but she tried, mainly to allow more time for Patrick to try to find her.

"Ok, so why did you have to kill them because of your dad?" she said it firmly but quietly.

"Oh Jodie do keep up." He returned to the photograph wall. "Whores, Jodie. They sleep with anything that will have them and my father was anything. You see, whores are one of the reasons that my dad became such an arsehole, he drank, took coke and had sex with dirty little *whores!*" He kept his eyes on the photographs of his victims.

"You think that Angela and the others deserved to die because you labelled them whores." Jodie could feel she was losing her temper, mainly because she was trying to keep Michelle's energy under control too.

"Well done Jodie, that's two out of two so far, you're getting the hang of this," he clapped sarcastically.

Jodie decided that the best tactic was to try to get him to think that she understood his mind, felt his pain and wanted to help him. So she began a dangerous game, one that if not played correctly, would end in her becoming number five on his victim list.

Forty Two

One step closer

Somehow, they had found themselves back at Patrick and Jodie's flat in Glasgow Harbour. Patrick didn't know what had drawn him to his home, but he knew that the spirits were leading him there, so he went with the instinct.

"So, now that we're here what do we do?" Lang whispered to Preston whilst Patrick was in the bathroom.

"I don't know. It's like trying to find a needle in a haystack I'll admit, but Patrick needs our support right now. And if you hadn't already realised, we have a missing person case!"

"You're damn right. We're missing one bloody killer." Lang was not at all being sarcastic. Preston was becoming irritated by Lang's constant need to criticise and mock Patrick, but he knew that now was not the time to bring it up again.

Patrick was sitting on the edge of the bath as Preston and Lang waited patiently in the lounge. He couldn't hear them whispering, he was too far away in his mind, watching the vision that was being played to him. He could see the car and which direction it was headed although the figure in the driving seat was a silhouette without a face. Patrick didn't recognise the car, but he did recognise the sticker on the back window, Kennedy and Clark Car and Van Hire.

That's the same company I hired our car from, he thought.

Now he was in the passenger seat, next to the driver. It felt so real that he wanted to reach over and punch the figure in the face. He could hear the sound of the tires on the road and he could hear the rush of the wind hitting the car as it travelled along the A82 back towards Glasgow. Patrick realised that this person must have followed him and Jodie to Lomond Park, even followed them to the car hire office. Did that mean that he had followed them from their flat?

"Patrick, we need to know our next move," Preston's voice jolted Patrick back to reality.

"I have something," he got up from the side of the bath and went into the kitchen. He took a card from the fridge door and showed it to Preston and Lang. "The guy followed us to Lomond Park and he was driving one of these cars."

Lang took the card from Patrick. "How do you suddenly know this?"

"I saw him driving a car back towards Glasgow, on the A82 and the car had this sticker on the back window," Patrick seemed so sure now.

Preston had no other choice but to believe him, they had absolutely no other leads and this seemed to be the closest that they were going to get. "Ok. So we go to the car hire office and ask for records of every car hire purchased two days ago, we narrow it down to the male drivers and investigate them."

"That will take too long," Patrick said.

"Listen Patrick, this is all we have, you're going to have to try and be patient. Let us do our job and you keep doing yours." Lang was beginning to doubt his scepticism once more, thinking the same as Preston was – this was all that they had to work on.

They rushed down the stairs of the building and leapt into Preston's car. As they made their journey to Kennedy and Clark Car and Van Hire, Patrick tried to stay as calm as he could. If he could sink into himself then maybe the spirits would show him the destination point of the car.

They pulled up outside of the hire office and made their way inside. The weather had taken a turn in the early afternoon and the sky was now bulging with thick, dark grey clouds that were releasing large blobs of cold rain. One dropped down onto Patrick's shoulder and as it soaked through his t-shirt he instantly felt the hairs on his left arm raise. He knew that it was not the rain that caused his skin to turn cold. Angela Noble was walking alongside him, quietly but with a heavy look of anxiousness on her face.

Preston and Lang disappeared inside the office and Patrick stayed outside, waiting for his message from Angela.

"You know him," was all she said.

"You have to tell me who it is," Patrick did speak aloud but only because he knew that there was nobody else around him.

"He is close to you now, but once was not," she showed him the image of the car again, further up the road that it travelled. Then he saw the image of Jodie, gagged and unconscious in the boot, unaware of her situation. It made bile rise to his throat but he swallowed it down.

"I don't understand. Once was not... what?" he watched the car as he tried to make sense of the words that she used.

He wracked his brain, searched in his mind to unravel the words that she used to describe the culprit.

"You mean I know him now, but haven't always? Is that it?" he asked but she was gone. The image of the car was also gone, but the colour of the car stuck in his memory.

He rushed into the office and could see that a woman in a blue and red shirt was taking them through files of paperwork.

"I've got more," Patrick called out as he approached the desk.

The woman looked up a little shocked at his sudden presence. She then looked at Preston who assured the woman that Patrick was a colleague.

"What do you have?" Lang asked.

"The car was black and I know him, but I haven't always known him," Patrick was beginning to sound a little panicked.

"Well, who do you know that you have only just met?" Lang asked him, almost sounding panicked himself.

Patrick thought about all of the people that he met for the first time since Angela had been murdered.

"Well, it could be anyone, I meet new people all of the time through the church," he paused. "And to be fair I have only known *you* two for a few weeks."

Lang let out a laugh that he couldn't control. "Get serious Patrick, police officers remember?"

Patrick didn't know who to trust, but he was certain that it must have been someone from the church as he didn't socialize that much out of work.

Then, he suddenly felt his body freeze, almost as if his muscles and joints had locked simultaneously. Preston watched the colour drain from Patrick's face. "What is it?"

He didn't want to believe it, but the situation would have been too much of a coincidence for it not to be true.

"Patrick, who?" Lang urged.

"Mark, it's Mark."

"What's the last name?"

"He didn't give me one, when he started working the shift at the bar, we just started talking and, I don't know, I just never thought to ask. And clearly he wasn't willing to give."

Lang shook his head. "Yeah and now we know why."

Preston asked the woman to look for the name Mark under a black car that was hired out on the day that Patrick hired out his.

"There is nobody under that name in any of the records sir," her voice was quivering.

Patrick was beginning to lose hope after a further thirty minutes of the woman searching her computer for a single name when she spoke. "I have found a booking that seems to be the only one that matches your requirements. It is a black Ford Focus one point nine turbo diesel, the only black car that we hired out that day."

"That's it, what's the name?" Patrick asked.

"A Mr Ross Turner," she said.

Patrick felt a wave on confusion was over him. "But how can that be?"

"I'm sorry sir that is the name that I have here," she said.

"It has to be correct, he would have had to produce a driving license to receive the car," Preston said.

"Can you make a note of that address please Miss?" Lang asked.

Patrick walked back outside, feeling defeated. He stood still, allowing the rain to soak him. Angela stood next to him once more, this time she smiled.

"What?" he asked aloud.

"You're nearly there, you have almost worked it out," she faded from his vision as she spoke. He took a deep breath, hoping and wishing that she was right.

"Ok, let's go," Preston said as he appeared in front of Patrick.

The three men got back into Preston's car and as he pulled out of the car park, Patrick felt the butterflies begin to swarm around the pit of his stomach as they began the journey to the address on the piece of paper.

Forty Three

The game

They had sat in silence for a long time. Jodie hadn't known which words to use to begin her dangerous game, so she decided that since she wasn't going anywhere, she would sit in silence.

Ross had paced the room in the time that no words were exchanged between the two, slow at times and quicker in others. She had been able to see his thoughts, some of them quite grim and sometimes she would only see little snippets. Michelle was allowing Jodie to see them but whenever Michelle got too angry her energy would rage and then flop and Jodie wouldn't see anything for a while.

Ross mainly thought of his mother, who Jodie now felt like she knew. Ross had run through his childhood a few times, unconsciously showing her the terrible abuse that Maria had suffered at the hands of Billy. She could see that Ross was seriously damaged by what he had seen as a child and in a way she felt sorry for him.

Grief can do terrible things to people, Rebecca said to Jodie.

Looks like it. His mother would be spinning in her grave if she could see him now, Jodie replied.

Trust me, she knows what he is doing. And deep down he knows that she would not be happy. But it's too late for him now, his time is up! Rebecca said in Jodie's mind.

What do you mean?

His grief has taken over his mind, it's going to kill him, Angela replied to Jodie's question.

Jodie watched Ross as he continued to walk back and forth, and at one point he stopped and closed the bedroom door. He looked over at Jodie, who quickly averted her eyes.

"You're quiet," he said.

"I was thinking about how similar we are."

There. She had said it, the game had begun.

"Ha!" he laughed loudly. "How the hell are we similar?"

"Well, I have never told anyone this but," she considered what she was going to say next before she said it, "my mum was abused too!"

He knitted his eyebrows as she spoke, he tried to read her words. "No chance, you're just saying that to get on side."

Jodie disregarded his words and continued. "It was awful, she was beaten on a daily basis by my Dad, her husband! I saw it, not every time, but I did hear it most times!" she spoke quietly, working from his own emotions inside his head. Although not exactly like his, she wasn't a raving lunatic!

"What did you do?" he found himself asking.

She felt the spirits willing her to go on, but carefully. "At first I used to try and stop it but then when he hit me, I would just to stay out of the way. I would put my headphones in or read."

Ross was wary of her words. He stood back, as if she was an unexploded bomb and he watched her. Was she playing, or was she showing him that he wasn't alone?

He smiled, which grew into a huge grin and then he laughed, "Ha, nice try Jodie but you are not fooling me. Good story teller, I'll give you that," he clapped again and returned to the wall.

"I get it you know," she continued as though she hadn't heard him speak.

"You don't get anything," he said quietly, irritation in his tone.

"When my Gran told me that I had to go and live with her because my Mum was dead, I knew then that I would never see my Dad again!" she managed to squeeze out a tear.

Ross did not reply, he kept his eyes on Patrick's photo.

"I never did see him again."

There was another bout of silence and Jodie was not sure what to do now. All of those words could either draw him in, make him lose his temper or simply do nothing.

"Where is he now?" he suddenly asked.

"Prison, he got twenty five years for murder," she felt her hands beginning to sweat from feeling so nervous.

"So why didn't you go and see him?" he seemed genuinely curious.

"Because my Gran wouldn't tell me what prison he was in and we moved away from where I was brought up. See, I am originally from Thurso, a small town up North..."

"Yes, I know where it is I'm not thick," he said annoyingly.

"Anyway, my Gran didn't want me growing up in a town where everyone would know me as the little girl whose Dad murdered her Mum, so she moved us down to Glasgow."

More silence...

"Doesn't it piss you off that you will never know what happened to your mum?" he asked.

"To be honest when I think about it, it makes me feel numb."

Ross sat down with his back against the wall. Now not only was he staring at her, but the faces of the spirits were too. She felt a lot of pressure building for her to pull through for everyone and she began to tremble.

"What are you doing?" Ross asked.

"I'm just cold. Sometimes this happens when I think about it," she was surprising herself. She was never one to tell lies, she just hoped that the lies would not trip her up later, if they worked at all.

"Well, deal with it. You might have parents that were fucked up like mine, but you are not getting any of my sympathy," he said harshly.

Jodie focused on calming down. She felt sleepy but tried to stay as alert as she could, she certainly did not want to fall asleep in the company of Ross.

Keep it quiet for now, he is considering your story and if you push it he will suss you out, Michelle said.

Jodie nodded inwardly and stayed quiet.

He made Jodie's skin crawl as she watched him play the murders over in his head. She could feel herself becoming distressed when she saw how he killed each one of them. She could feel his hands around her own neck and she could feel the panic that *they* must have felt when he was killing them.

What she saw in his mind next made her feel sick. She watched his imagination play out the scene of strangling her, in the very room in which they sat.

She got up and ran for the small bin in the opposite corner to where she was. She was violently sick into it but due to an empty stomach, all that surfaced was bile which made her wretch even more.

Before she had a chance to compose herself, she realised that Ross was standing over her holding a tall glass with water in it. "Here," he said as he handed it to her.

She reluctantly took the glass from his hand and instinctively began to sniff the liquid.

"It's pure H2O, no Chloroform for you now. Well, not right now anyway," he sat back down at the wall.

"Is that what you used to get me here?" Jodie felt the rage begin to boil along with her bubbling stomach, but she had just enough energy left to cool it back down.

"That and a car," he smirked. "Oh, I almost forgot. I switched your sleeping tablets for stronger ones. I hope you don't mind, it made getting you here a lot easier."

Jodie gulped at the water until the glass was empty, desperately pushing his words out of her head. "Why did you take me?" she asked.

"Because, he was ruining it!" he raised his voice.

"Patrick?" she knew that was who he meant.

He kept his head low, but raised his eyes when he looked at Jodie, "He was going to stop me from taking my girls. The ones who deserve to die, so I decided to take his from him."

Forty Four

The last piece of the puzzle

The journey to the address felt like it was being taken in slow motion. Patrick clutched his knees with his hands as he looked out of the window and all that he could think of was what he would find on his arrival. He knew that Jodie could die tonight and he knew it well. What would happen to him then? He couldn't bare to answer that question.

"So, why is it that you don't have the same name as the one that we were given back at the hire place?" Lang asked from the front seat.

"I don't know but now that you mention it the name is really familiar," Patrick massaged his temples.

"Oh?" Preston looked at Patrick in the rear mirror to see his face turn a shade of grey.

"Oh my god," Patrick said quietly.

"What?" Lang turned to him.

Patrick pulled a letter from the inside pocket of his jacket and unfolded it. His eyes darted back and forth as he read and Lang watched him, wondering what was going to come from his mouth next.

"Pull over, quick!" Patrick shouted.

Preston pulled into the side of the road and Patrick threw the door open and began vomiting onto the pavement.

"Urgh! What the hell!" Lang got out of the car and tried to compose himself. The sound of Patrick's stomach contents hitting the ground caused a stir in Lang's stomach.

He finally emptied his stomach and got out of the car for some air. Preston met him on the pavement and asked, "What is it Patrick?"

"I have something to tell you," Patrick said, "but not on the street, let's get back in the car and I will tell you on the way to the address, we need to get there right now."

As they climbed back in the car Lang averted his eyes from the vomit on the ground and he closed the door.

"Right, what is it?" Preston asked as he started the car again.

Patrick took the deepest breath possible and began to speak. "Ok, there is one thing that I never told you both about me. I am adopted."

"What the hell has that got to do with this?" Lang asked.

"Just listen to me!" Patrick snapped.

"Ok, before we go any further we all need to stay calm for Jodie's sake here," Preston added without taking his eyes off the road. "I will put my siren on so that..."

"No," Patrick said. "He will know that we are on our way and doing that will only allow him time to get away."

"Ok, ok I will keep it off."

"As I said, I am adopted and up until last year I was happy not knowing where I had come from. Years ago I had put my name on a database allowing my biological parents to contact me if they wanted too but they never did." Patrick could feel tears building in his eyes with what he was about to say next.

"Go on," Lang said with interest.

"I received a letter from a place called Adoption Contact Scotland last year and it was from my biological brother. One that I did not know existed. It took me six months to reply and a lot of thought went into whether or not I wanted to meet him. But in the end I decided that I didn't have anything to lose and I agreed."

Preston looked in the mirror at Patrick and saw that he had real fear in his eyes. "What happened? How is this connected to the case?"

Patrick raised his hand to his mouth, the shock of the whole situation was beginning to hit him. "The name that the woman at the hire place gave us is the name of my biological brother."

"Ross Turner? That's a very common name Patrick it could be a complete coincidence," Lang said.

"No, it is not a coincidence. You may not believe in what I do Lang, but I am telling you now, this case was meant to come to me. I am the only person that can stop him."

Preston stopped the car.

"We're here," said Lang.

"Now what?" Preston asked.

***

He has figured it out, Angela said to the others.

Good. It is about time we all put an end to this, Michelle growled.

We still have a lot to get Jodie through, he is so unpredictable at this point that his plans could change before we see it. We all have to be very careful what we say to him through Jodie.

Michelle and Rebecca swirled around Ross as he stood at the door of the bedroom watching Jodie. He did not believe in spirits and afterlife, which for the girls was a good thing. What they had planned would hopefully scare him enough into shock and give Jodie the chance to escape.

Whatever happens in here tonight, we cannot let there be a fifth death, Rebecca said.

Jodie had heard the whole conversation in her head as she watched Ross, watching her, planning his next move.

Agreed, Jodie said, allowing only them to hear it. They put all of their energies together to protect her.

Ross had been silent for a while and hadn't said anything to Jodie since he said that he was going to take Patricks girl. He had been thinking of the best way to tell Jodie about the adoption situation. He wanted to say it with perfection so that he could see the look on her face before he committed murder number five and then end his own life. He knew that his time was almost up before the police caught up with him and he wasn't going to prison to stare at four walls for the rest of his days. That would really drive him insane, being stuck inside a prison cell with his thoughts for years to come and no way of releasing the pain.

"You know, I know something about your psychic man, something very personal," he said.

Jodie looked up from the floor where she was sitting and saw a look on his face that said he had won. "And what is that?" she asked.

"I know about Jeffrey," he sneered.

Jodie felt her blood run cold at the sound of that name. "Jeffrey?" she tried to control the tremble in her voice. "How do you know about that?"

Ross smiled and walked toward her, intensifying the pause before he sat down on the floor beside her. "Oh, I have been doing my research."

Jodie tried to think of anything that would make her understand his knowledge of Jeffrey. "Did Patrick tell you about his adoption when you and he were working together? Or should I say Patrick and Mark?" she said sarcastically.

"Ah, Mark. Quite a character don't you think? I am quite proud of him, he has created quite an ending scene for us," he smiled widely, rubbing his hands together.

Jodie shivered at his creepiness as he continued to speak. "No he didn't tell me about Jeffrey, my Mum did actually." He looked at her, expecting confusion.

"You're Mum? How did she know him?" Jodie searched her own mind for the answer but only heard Angela.

Stay calm Jodie.

"Because Jodie, we share the same blood. Turner blood," he said with a sneer.

"What? I don't understand?"

Ross jumped to his feet and said, "Brothers, Jodie. We are biological brothers. My Mum gave him up for adoption when she had him, my Dad made her do it. Good thing for him I suppose, he escaped the evil clutches my Dad."

Jodie couldn't believe what she was hearing. "How do you know that Patrick is your biological brother? How long have you known?"

"Now Jodie one question at a time," he patronisingly patted her on the head. He was jumping around like a hyperactive child on Christmas morning after revealing his information. "I know he is my biological brother because when my Mum died she left a box for me to find. In that box was a letter to me and a letter to Jeffrey. I read the one to Jeffrey first, I guess the reason was because she wanted me to read it first, you see it was the first letter at the top of the box. Underneath that one was the letter addressed to me. I was so confused at first, I mean how couldn't I have known about him? But she kept it from me to protect me," he spoke so passionately about his Mum that Jodie was beginning to see why her death had driven him insane, to the point of murder.

"Go on," she said, trying to swallow down the bile that was rising from her stomach.

"You see, she almost gave me away too. But she fought him, for me," he smiled. "She left him but he managed to claw his way back in. If she had been brave enough to say no then maybe you wouldn't be in this situation Jodie."

"But I am," she said. She could feel herself rising.

"Don't even think about it. I am not finished with you yet," he said as he pushed her back down.

Let him finish, you need to hear this, Angela said to her.

It wasn't Jodie who stood up, it was me, Michelle replied.

Keep your cool Michelle. You can have him soon. Patrick is on his way.

"He's found us?" Jodie said aloud.

Ross took a step back from Jodie. "Oh has he now?" he smiled.

Jodie stayed silent as she tried to listen for Patrick's thoughts. She could hear Michelle in her mind, she was pumped full of energy and ready to take revenge on Ross. She could hear Angela trying to relax Michelle's energy and Rebecca silently circling Ross. Anna took Michelle's place so that they could put their energies together and protect Jodie for when the time came.

Jodie kept her eyes on Ross as he continued to speak of his Mum and Jeffrey. She heard the car pull up outside, but Ross didn't. She had heard it through Patrick's mind. She kept her eyes on him as he continued to justify what he had been doing and why he had to do it. So much was going on around her and in her head that she was struggling to make it look as though she was really listening to him.

"Hey, you better be keeping up with me. I need you to know all of this so that you can tell psychic boy when you contact him from the dead!" he sniggered.

Jodie nodded.

Here they come, said Angela.

Jodie couldn't hide the smile on her face.

Forty Five

Game over

"I can hear her," Patrick said as he, Preston and Lang sat in the car outside Ross Turner's flat.

"You can?" Lang sounded surprised.

"Yeah, I can hear all of them," he concentrated.

Preston turned to Patrick and asked, "Who?"

"Jodie, Angela, Michelle, Rebecca, Anna. I can even hear him," he replied through gritted teeth at the last word.

Preston got out of the car and Lang followed. Before they knew it Patrick was already standing next to the buzzer.

"Don't go wading in there before we have discussed this Patrick," Lang said.

Patrick put a hand on Lang's shoulder, "You're police officers aren't you?"

"Yes, so let us handle this," Preston said.

"Trust me on this one, you need to call for back up right now. Jodie is telling me what is in that flat. He has pictures of the girls on the wall that he murdered, news paper cuttings, dates... the lot!"

Preston ran his hand over his face, "Are you one hundred percent sure about this Patrick?"

"I am one million percent sure. If I am wrong, then shoot me!"

Lang fell back against the wall and looked at Preston, "I say we call for back up and go in."

"You have a gun?" Patrick asked.

"What do you think this is, an American cop film?" Preston replied.

"No, we have batons and spray, which is more than enough considering that there are three of us," Lang added.

Patrick listened to Jodie as she spoke to Ross.

***

"You think that your precious psychic boy has found us?" Ross asked.

"I don't know. But if he hasn't it won't be long before he does," Jodie replied.

She knew that Patrick was outside with Preston and Lang but she had no idea what they were going to do.

"Yeah, and by then it will be too late," he sniggered.

Jodie hadn't heard Ross' comment for the conversation going on in her head. Any sudden movement from outside and Ross could kill her right there in the very room he had kept her hostage in, which had now been fifteen hours.

My god, has it been that long? She said to herself, noticing the small clock on the wall.

Yes it has. Not much longer to go. We are going to do everything to get you out of here Jodie, Angela replied.

Angela was acting like a guardian angel to Jodie, although she knew that when the time came, she and the others were going to harm Ross to the point of no return.

An eye for an eye Jodie, that is what this is all about. He wants revenge for his mother's death and we want revenge for ours, Rebecca said as she and Anna continued to circle Ross.

They did not look like their past human form as they encircled Ross in a cloudy mist. At points where their energies fought against his anger Jodie struggled to see him as their mist became thicker and darker.

"Don't you ever worry about what will happen to your soul once you are dead?" Jodie asked. This was one of her questions, not one of the spirits. Ross regarded this for a moment.

"I would like to think that I will see my Mum when I die," he looked up as he spoke.

Jodie knew the next comment she was about to make was a dangerous one. "But your Mum won't be in hell surely. I mean, she sounded like a good woman, she would be in heaven for sure."

"What did you say?" he narrowed his eyes and moved towards her.

"You heard, I said that your Mum will be in heaven. You are going to hell Ross."

He hurtled towards her, fist clenched and teeth gritted. Jodie stood her ground, she knew that he couldn't hurt her. He fell to the floor as the pain in his head pierced through his brain. He yelped like a dog.

Ross held his head as he clumsily climbed to his feet and when he looked at Jodie his eyes were glazed over like ice, colder than she had ever seen them.

"Time's up," he said as he left the room.

"Where's he going?" Jodie whispered into the room.

He has gone to the kitchen, Angela said.

"Why? What is he doing?" Jodie was beginning to panic.

Something bad is going to happen. We need to get you out now, Angela said.

"Where are Rebecca and Anna, are they still circling him?"

Yes but their energies are running low. You have to get Patrick up here now.

Jodie could hear Ross making a lot of noise from the kitchen and she was petrified at what he was going to do. Would he appear with a knife?

She sent her thoughts down to Patrick, who had already been listening to everything that had been happening.

What do I do now? Time is running out Patrick. Do something!

Don't worry. The girls are taking care of it, he replied.

Just then, Ross appeared in the doorway of the room and in his hand was nothing but a lighter. "Now all we do is wait."

"Wait for what?" Jodie asked.

"I was thinking it is a little cold in here. I have just turned on the gas, the fire will be along any minute now." He tossed the lighter in the air and caught it with his other hand.

Jodie thought of the dream, the burning of her skin, the fire around her and the smoke.

"You had this planned right from the start didn't you?"

"Entirely," he replied.

***

"We need to make a move right now or that flat is going to explode," Patrick said.

"What? How do you know that?" Lang asked bewildered.

"Jodie is sending me her thoughts and I heard him say that he has turned on the gas to get the fire going."

Patrick was just about to push the buzzer when an elderly lady opened the entrance door to the building. "Oh, looks like I was just in time," she smiled at them.

"Oh please, ladies first," Preston said, returning the smile.

The woman walked down the street away from the building. "Good thing she is leaving," Patrick said.

"Let me go first," Preston said. He walked slowly as he made his way up the stairs to Ross' front door.

"Jesus, the place is oozing gas," Lang said.

"Quiet," Patrick hissed. "If he hears us now, he will flick that lighter and we will all go up."

They reached the front door and Patrick's mind was going wild with the amount of voices in the flat.

"One at a time please," he whispered.

"I didn't say anything." Lang said.

"Not you, you idiot," Preston replied. "He's talking to them."

Lang couldn't help but feel like they were all on a wild goose chase and worried that there would be nothing and no one in the flat they were approaching. Even after everything that had happened, he felt the scepticism set in once more.

Patrick stood a step up from the front door and Preston and Lang a second and third so that if Ross did hear anything then looking through the spy hole, he wouldn't see anyone.

***

Distract him, Angela said to Michelle.

Jodie felt Michelle's spirit leave the room as Ross paced the floor. There was a low hissing sound coming from the kitchen. It was the sound of gas being released from the hobs on the cooker.

"What are you going to do?" Jodie asked.

"I told you, we are going to have a little barbecue," he smiled.

"But why?" Jodie was beginning to lose her nerve and she could feel the tears beginning to take over.

"Aww," he taunted. "Is this the part where you are going to beg for your life? Are you going to tell me I can have your money and you won't tell the police?" he laughed loudly but was interrupted by a bumping sound from the kitchen.

He slowly walked into the kitchen and looked around. Something wasn't right.

"The hobs are off!" he said aloud, puzzled by it.

Jodie had heard him from the bedroom but did not reply.

He turned to walk back into the room when the lighter was suddenly knocked from his hand and he was thrown to the other side of the hallway. Jodie could hear the growling sound from Michelle getting louder and as she stood up and walked to the bedroom door she also heard a loud bang. She peered around the door and saw that Ross was lying down on the kitchen floor holding his ribs.

Michelle had thrown her energy at Ross and he was knocked to the ground, banging his ribs on the worktop as he had gone down.

Jodie ran back to the wall of the bedroom where Ross' collection of pictures and other things were gathered together and she pulled them down carefully but quickly. She kept her eyes on the door as she folded them in one pile and held onto them tight.

There came another bang but this time it came from the front door.

Forty Six

Going out with a Bang

Preston kicked with all of the force that he could and with every kick he could feel the door becoming weak under the impact. It only took four attempts before the door gave way and the Yale lock released. Before he knew it he was inside the entrance hallway of Ross Turner's flat and he could see that Ross was stood in the doorway of the kitchen which faced the front door directly. Patrick was behind Lang and the last one inside the flat.

Both officers held their batons extended away from their bodies and Ross was standing facing them. "Police, drop your weapon!" Preston shouted.

Patrick ran into the room that was to the left of him and he saw Jodie standing inside, rooted to the spot. There was a stench of gas in the air.

"Come on, we need to get out of here and leave them to deal with the rest of this. You're not safe," Patrick said as he held her upper arm to guide her out.

"None of us are safe. We all have to get out now before they begin," Jodie said with tears in her eyes. "They had turned the hobs off to distract him, but they have turned them back on again and they plan to set this place off Patrick."

Patrick noticed the pile of paper under her other arm but did not comment on it, he just continued to pull her towards the door. They reached the hallway and could hear the sirens coming from the street.

"They called for backup," Patrick said.

Get out now! Michelle shouted in Jodie's head, Patrick had heard it too.

"Preston we have to leave right now," Jodie said.

Ross had not moved from the minute the door had been kicked in. He stood completely still in the kitchen, holding the lighter in his hand (which he had retrieved from the floor before getting up) and was looking straight ahead.

"He hasn't moved an inch," Lang said.

"It's Michelle, her energy is holding him there. He is paralysed by her," Patrick said. "Jodie is right we need to leave now or we are all going to be burnt alive."

Preston and Lang hesitated, "We need to take this man into questioning. We're not leaving without him," Lang said with confusion in his tone.

Even after all the weeks working with Patrick he still couldn't bring himself to believe that everything that had happened was true and Patrick had been right the whole time.

"If you have never trusted me before just trust me now, we *have* to leave," Patrick was now shouting.

Preston was still standing face to face with Ross, unsure of what was about to happen but knowing that Patrick and Jodie's words were not spoken lightly. "OK, let's go," he said, backing out of the kitchen slowly not turning his back on Ross. The smell of gas was getting stronger.

"Hey Jeffrey?" Ross called out.

Patrick stopped dead in his tracks and let go of Jodie's arm. He turned to face Ross and walked towards him.

Leave now Patrick, he heard Michelle say. Her voice was rough, angry and it rang in his ears.

"Is it really you?" Patrick almost whispered. He tried to push out the sight of Michelle holding Ross on the spot while the other girl's spirits surrounded him.

Jodie knew that she should have sent Patrick the message about Ross before hand but she had wanted to tell him in person.

"Absolutely, nice to meet you brother," Ross was still portraying his arrogant cockiness even though Michelle had disabled any physical movement. His evil smile spread across his face, from ear to ear and emanated cruelty.

"Why?" was all that Patrick could get out. He had never been called Jeffrey before, that he could of remember anyway. It felt odd and coming from a cold blooded killer it sent shivers down his spine.

"Because Jeffrey. Our mother killed herself," he said, the sourness leaving his face.

"You are a sick bastard!"

"No, I am angry. You got out Jeffrey, and I had to endure a life of pain. It just so happens that my mother left a box of letters for me and you when she died. I wanted to find you, try to build a relationship. But you see, I can't let it go."

Patrick felt a great wave of sadness wash over him but he didn't know who he felt sad for. "Let what go?"

"Mum's death, someone had to pay. Dad's dead, so the only ones left to pay are the whores that walk this world, wrecking lives."

"That's no excuse!" Patrick shouted.

"You know nothing about it. You didn't have to go through it! Well, when I sent those papers away and I saw that you were Jeffrey my plan for us changed."

Patrick knew instantly that there were three men standing in front of him at this point, a murderer, Mark and his brother... Ross Turner.

"You can't hurt anyone anymore," Patrick turned his back to see Jodie standing at the open front door holding a box now.

"We need to leave right now!" Jodie exclaimed.

The space around Ross was turning black and there was a terrible, low growling sound coming from the kitchen. Preston ushered Patrick out the door quickly. He looked back at the man standing in the kitchen, who could not move. "Bye Ross, Mark... whoever you are."

"Just remember Jeffrey," Ross' voice now trembled and Patrick was becoming overwhelmed by the smell of gas, "we share the same blood, the same parents. We are Turners and that is why you are scared!" Ross was shouting out and Patrick could hear fear now.

"I'm a McLaughlin. The only thing that we share right now is the knowledge that you are going to burn to your death here, then you will burn in hell forever."

Preston slammed the door and the last image in Patrick's mind was Ross, stood in his kitchen, alone and about to go up in flames.
***

Ross watched as the bolts on the door began locking themselves. He could feel the floor shake slightly and he could feel heaviness on his chest. As he looked around, he noticed that there was an eerie silence in the flat. A mist was descending from above him and it was making him feel sick.

"This isn't the way it was supposed to be!" he screamed out, clenching his fists. His eyes darted back and forth as Michelle appeared slowly in front of him. He watched her appear like a fade- in edit on a film. She looked almost exactly like she did after he had killed her but this time she was moving.

"You're damn right this wasn't the way things were supposed to happen," she growled in his ear.

Ross had turned grey and there was sweat dripping from his brows. He tried to move, even just a finger. But it was no use. "You're ours now," Anna said from behind him.

Angela and Rebecca were with him now and he watched unwillingly as they swirled around him and taunted him.

"So, looks like he was right, my brother. Ghosts *are* real." Ross gave his last twisted smile. "Rot in hell!" he hissed at them.

Michelle smiled with redness in her eyes that told him this was the end. "No Ross, you will."

The bang was so loud and the heat was so hot that Ross knew nothing about it. His death came in an instant.

Forty Seven

Three months later

Jodie gazed at herself in the mirror and felt the overwhelming happiness make the butterflies flutter once more in her stomach. She patted down her dress and touched up her make-up before leaving the bedroom. "Are your eyes closed?" she called out.

"Shut tight," Patrick called back.

Jodie took a deep breath and walked into the living room. The autumn sun shone through the glass doors as it had began to set and it gave an orange glow to the room. She placed herself in the doorway and took another breath. "OK, open them."

Patrick opened his eyes and when he saw her he instantly fell in love again. The sun made her face shine and the dress was simple, showing of her slender shape and the beauty that Patrick loved so much. "You look like a lady that I would marry," he said with a grin.

"Well then it is a good thing that I had this lying around. I am free now if you're up for it?"

"I would be honoured."

Patrick took Jodie's hand gently in his and they walked down the stairs of their building for the last time as Patrick McLaughlin and Jodie Jenkins.

***

As they danced their first dance as a married couple, Jodie held on tight as Patrick took the lead. The restaurant was dimly lit with the piano playing softly in the background and their small selections of guests were gathered round them.

"So, Mrs McLaughlin, how does it feel to be my wife?" Patrick smiled gently as they swayed to the soft notes.

"It feels pretty good if I am honest. Who would have known after everything that happened that we would be here today," she said with glazed eyes.

Patrick pulled her closer. "I told you I would never let anything bad happen to you and I will live my life to that vow until the day I die." He kissed her gently and they continued to dance.

"Are you going to open it?" she asked, referring to the box Jodie had taken from Ross' flat.

"I have been thinking about it. Everything happened so fast, finding out about Ross, how my birth parents lives were such a mess. I had a whole other family out there that was a complete mess and I find out about it because the murderer, who turned out to be first of all my friend Mark who wasn't real, followed us to the cottage, kidnapped you, I turn up to rescue you and find that he is, in actual fact my biological brother."

"I understand if you are not ready and I understand why you didn't tell me you were in contact with the adoption people. I just want you to know that in future, we tell each other everything. After all, we are Mr and Mrs McLaughlin now." she smiled.

Patrick kissed Jodie again. "I will not argue with that."
***

Jodie lay in bed fast asleep. Their wedding day had been an amazing day but an exhausting one. As she lay there, Patrick watched her sleep. She still looked beautiful as he watched her chest rise and fall with every breath she took.

Patrick got up from the bed and went in to the living room. The box had been sitting on the floor in the corner of the room for months and he just couldn't bring himself to open it.

He wasn't even sure if he wanted to open it. What he would find wouldn't change the fact that his life had been turned upside down by a monster who he now knew was his biological brother.

He understood now what his Grandpa had meant when he said all those years ago that he would understand that he had a purpose. Patrick was *meant* to stop Ross.

He continued to stare at the box and he felt it stare back at him. *Open it.*

Patrick looked up to see a woman standing at the opposite side of the room. It was Maria Turner.

Go on. Open it, you'll never know if you don't.

Patrick pulled the box towards him and he sat on the floor. He gently lifted the lid.

There was a photo of him as a baby, with his birth name and date on the back, letters, birthday cards and more.

Patrick searched through them all, reading the letters from Maria to him and from Maria to Ross. He was mesmerised but sad at the same time.

"Now I understand why he was so angry," he whispered to himself.

It does not excuse what he did, Maria replied.

"You know, I had a life before this and I almost lost it because of him. Nothing inside this box is going to change that. I am still Patrick and I will never be Jeffrey. I am sorry if that is hard for you to hear but if none of this had happened I would not know anything about you."

Maria nodded, *I understand. I came to say sorry for what has happened.*

Patrick did not say anymore. There was nothing too say.

She was gone.

Forty Eight

One month after the wedding

Preston closed the file that was stamped, 'Ross Turner' and pushed it aside. He sighed a relieved sigh and looked across the desk at Patrick. "Case closed. Ross Turner is dead and all the evidence that we gathered from the materials Jodie handed to us from the flat proves that he was the only person involved in the murders."

Patrick nodded. "You're giving me good cause to go out and buy a very expensive bottle of champagne Preston, thank you. Although, I still don't think there is cause for celebration, four women have died because of him. If anything we should have a drink in their honour."

Lang was stood beside Preston. He nodded and said, "I don't disagree with that."

"At least we can now rest and know that he cannot cause anymore grief to any other families, including yours," Preston said to Patrick.

"Speaking of family, how was the wedding?" Lang asked.

"It was perfect and just what we needed after everything that has happened."

Lang smiled and sat down on the chair next to Preston. "Should we tell him now?"

Patrick knitted his eyebrows. "Tell me what?"

Preston opened the drawer to his right and slid a brown envelope across the table which had Patrick's name on it.

"What's this?" he asked curiously.

"It's a contract," Lang replied.

"The boss was so impressed with what you helped us to achieve Patrick. We had no leads and you led us right to him, yeah OK, it took a little time and a lot of convincing on Lang's part," he rolled his eyes, "but you really pulled through for the case."

Patrick looked down at the envelope and then back to Preston and Lang. "So what are you saying?"

"We're saying the boss wants you on our team. He has had a contract drawn up that has certain policies and stipulations in place. It states that you will work with us on murder inquiries, missing person cases and generally cases like we have just seen. Your title will be specialist liaison officer and you will work with any officers within this region who need your assistance. All you have to do is sign." Lang said.

Patrick laughed. "Lang, I would have thought you would want rid of me after the case was closed."

Lang stood up and walked around the table to Patrick's side. "Well, if I could have it my way." he said sarcastically. "No, seriously I am holding my hands up. You did a great job." Lang held out his hand and Patrick shook it.

Preston rested his hands behind his head and gently swirled his chair from left to right. "So, what do you say Patrick, are you in?"

Made in the USA
Charleston, SC
06 June 2014